Sarah

Texts and Translations

The Texts and Translations series was founded in 1991 to provide students and teachers with important texts not readily available or not available at an affordable price and in high-quality translations. The books in the series are intended for students in upper-level undergraduate and graduate courses in national literatures in languages other than English, comparative literature, ethnic studies, area studies, translation studies, women's studies, and gender studies. The Texts and Translations series is overseen by an editorial board composed of specialists in several national literatures and in translation studies.

For a complete listing of titles, see the last pages of this book.

MARCELINE DESBORDES-VALMORE

Sarah
An English Translation

Translated by
Deborah Jenson and Doris Y. Kadish

The Modern Language Association of America
New York   2008

©2008 by The Modern Language Association of America
All rights reserved
Printed in the United States of America

For information about obtaining permission to reprint material from
MLA book publications, send your request by mail (see address below),
e-mail (permissions@mla.org), or fax (646 458-0030).

Library of Congress Cataloging-in-Publication Data
Desbordes-Valmore, Marceline, 1786–1859.
[Sarah. English]
Sarah : an English translation / Marceline Desbordes-Valmore ;
translated by Deborah Jenson and Doris Kadish.
p. cm. — (Texts and translations. Translations ; 22)
Includes bibliographical references.
ISBN 978-1-60329-027-2 (pbk. : alk. paper)
I. Jenson, Deborah. II. Kadish, Doris Y. III. Title.
PQ2218.D75S313 2008
843'.7—dc22   2008023271

Texts and Translations 22
ISSN 1079-2538

Cover illustration: *Plantation Slave House*, from Pierre Jacques Benoit's
Voyage à Surinam (1839). Used with permission of the John Carter Brown
Library at Brown University

Printed on recycled paper

Published by The Modern Language Association of America
26 Broadway, New York, New York 10004-1789
www.mla.org

CONTENTS

INTRODUCTION

Marceline Desbordes-Valmore (1786–1859) is a major figure in French Romanticism. Her novella about slavery, entitled *Sarah* (1821), has garnered significantly less attention than her poetic oeuvre, however, despite the dramatic circumstances that form its background.

In 1802, the teenaged actress Desbordes-Valmore and her mother, Catherine (who was estranged from her husband), set sail for Guadeloupe, ostensibly to seek financial assistance from well-to-do relatives. But when they arrived, the port was closed because of military and economic tensions associated with revolutionary upheaval in the French Caribbean. The ship found a welcoming harbor on the politically neutral island of Saint-Barthélemy, where the two women made friends among the Creole population during their three-month stay. In May, when they were at last allowed to enter Guadeloupe, their arrival coincided not only with a yellow fever epidemic but also with a rebellion among the black population. The rebellion followed the news that Napoléon Bonaparte planned to reinstitute slavery there, eight years after its formal abolition under the French

Revolution. Desbordes-Valmore experienced the chaos of a historical moment torn between revolutionary idealism on the rights of man and the imperialist ideology of the Napoleonic era. Catherine succumbed to yellow fever and died at around the same time that former slaves, cornered by French soldiers on a mountaintop, ignited a massive explosion, killing hundreds on both sides. The leader in that episode, Louis Delgrès, had issued a proclamation begging future generations to recognize the plight of the blacks. Addressed "To the Entire Universe" as a "Cry of Innocence and Despair," it spoke of "a class of unfortunates who are threatened with destruction, and find themselves forced to raise their voices so that posterity will know, once they have disappeared, of their innocence and misery" (Dubois 391–92).

In *Sarah*, set in Saint-Barthélemy, Desbordes-Valmore mingles the theme of personal bereavement with the theme of the tragedy of slavery. The motherless and illegitimate heroine, Sarah, feels that a male former slave, Arsène, is a mother to her. Although Sarah appears (and is) white, the plot hinges on moments of uncertainty concerning her free or enslaved status, just as Arsène's own status fluctuates between freedom and reenslavement. Through this model of the maternal male slave and the idea of a vulnerability to slavery that crosses color lines, Desbordes-Valmore broadens the scope of identification in existing literary representations of slavery. Like her peer Claire de Duras in *Ourika* (1823), she approaches the problem of slavery not directly, through discussion of history and politics, but indirectly, through the affective and interpersonal vulnerability of a human family. This thematic approach does not make *Sarah* ahistorical, however. The threats of Arsène's reenslavement and Sarah's enslavement metaphorically reflect the reality of former slaves' ambiguous freedom in Guadeloupe after the 1794 abolition and their impending formal reenslavement in 1802. Desbordes-Valmore melds the loss of her mother in Guadeloupe in May 1802 with the loss of freedom that former slaves were resisting in the same place and time. *Sarah* thus recognizes the plight of the revolutionary Caribbean in 1802 as urged by Delgrès in his proclamation.

Desbordes-Valmore's personal background differs from many well-known women writers of the late eighteenth and early nineteenth century, such as Germaine de Staël and Duras, whose experience and writing are rooted in the elite culture of the French salon. In contrast, the life of Desbordes-Valmore places her closer to the social margins negotiated in *Sarah*. Linguistically, her background was not foreign to that of Creole speakers in the French Caribbean. Although born in Douai, the capital of Flanders, which had been part of France since 1667, she was nostalgically attached to Flemish customs. She called the Flemish "patois" that appears in several of her poems the language "that I still stammer in my heart, just as when I was a little thing" (*Œuvres* 2: 785).[1] Later, when she was stranded in Saint-Barthélemey, she learned elements of Creole sufficiently to publish two poems in a Creole-French hybrid ("Le réveil créole" and "Tournez, tournez cher' belle" [585, 619]).[2] Throughout her life, then, Desbordes-Valmore found herself situated between regional and official languages as well as between the language of the cultural elite and the popular language of the majority.

Economically, the author of *Sarah* also stood on the margins. Her father, Antoine-Félix Desbordes, an artisanal painter whose livelihood shifted during the Revolution to a variety of unfortunate business schemes, repeatedly placed his family in financial jeopardy. His selling her brother in 1800 as a replacement for a military conscript indicates an eerie congruency between the lives of lower-income whites and blacks at the time. Subsequently, both her father and brother would rely on her to support them for much of their lives. Her sisters, Cécile and Eugénie, led the precarious lives of unwed mothers. Yet the uncertain circumstances of Marceline's background, which Marceline shared with other women of her class, did not preclude a degree of empowerment. Consider the women in her immediate family. Although by marrying an artisan, Catherine presumably rose above her lower-class rank, in fact the marriage was an unhappy one; the only real elevation in her status appears to have come from her own efforts and those of other women with whom she came in contact. Illiterate when she married Antoine-Félix in 1776, she managed to learn to read, despite the domestic burdens of bearing and caring for children. Assisted in her self-education by her sister-in-law, Thérèse Sagé, and other educated women, Catherine came to love literature and made it a part of her children's upbringing. Thérèse also provided instruction to Cécile Desbordes, who in turn taught Marceline to read. At a time when education was neither free nor available to girls, women teaching other women could be a ticket out of impoverishment and oppression, as it was for blacks who received instruction from whites and from their more educated peers. Later in her life, Marceline, the godmother of Eugénie's daughter Camille, encouraged her niece's education, advising Camille to learn to spell by copying great works, as she herself had done.

Another important circumstance in the life of the women of the Desbordes family that may have influenced the author's openness to people outside white bourgeois culture is the extent to which they failed to conform to bourgeois standards of domesticity and submission to male authority. Inspired by friends who either divorced or left their marriages when divorce became possible in 1792, Catherine ran off with a lover in 1795, taking Marceline with her. When Catherine's lover proved to be no more financially dependable than her husband, Catherine and her daughter were reduced to living hand to mouth and often faced destitution.

In fact, although Desbordes-Valmore always explained her trip to the Caribbean as a visit to relatives, those relatives were never found, and according to Francis Ambrière they may not have existed (1: 102–03). The history of theater in the French Caribbean, in which many actors, including those who spoke parts with Creole dialogue, were European, suggests that the two women may have been seeking theatrical employment in a colonial context.

Yet Catherine's example of financial self-sufficiency appears to have been viewed in positive terms by her daughter. Writing to a friend in 1812, at a time when her hopes for marriage and respectability had just been dashed, Marceline stated:

May my fate be a useful lesson for you. Never turn over the responsibility for your existence to a man, however much he may love you. Be independent, and only rely on your talents in preparing for the future. Circumstances change, and even the most honorable of men change with them.

(Ambrière 1: 165)

Although married to Prosper Valmore from 1817 until her death in 1859,[3] Marceline followed the example of her mother and sisters in having several liaisons and bearing illegitimate children. A reputation for loose morals was not unique to her. Other literary or artistic women who adopted nontraditional roles—her sometime friend, the author Sophie Gay, is an example—similarly chose or were forced to situate themselves outside conventional, patriarchal society.[4]

The marginalized world of the theater, in which Catherine Desbordes passed on her lessons of strength and survival to Marceline, was a favored locus for feminine independence and empowerment, a locus that offered great resources for persons, male and female, whose difficult family situations required that they rely on themselves. In addition to enabling women from destabilized personal backgrounds to lead independent lives, the world of the theater placed them in contact with the urgent political and social issues of their time: "Ever since the closing of churches, the theater was the only place where people could assemble in sufficient number to form a sounding board whose political significance did not go unnoticed" (Ambrière 1: 70–71). Having learned about opportunities in the theater, Catherine chose to place her daughter on the stage at age eleven. Afterward, the newly formed family unit of Catherine, her lover, and Marceline moved from city to city, subjected to the vagaries of their employment by a variety of theater directors. Although economically and geographically unstable, this world was not without its advantages for Marceline as a young girl. She was immersed in literature through learning parts and performing roles from dramatic texts on the stage. She was exposed to powerful women in the theater and their skills at maintaining networks and control of the conditions of their professional lives: Jeanne Larivau, a theater director in Bayonne; Mme Duversin, the leader of the troupe to which Marceline belonged; Mme Saint-Aubin, a great star and central force in decisions about all theatrical matters affecting those around her.

These various forms of marginality in the early life of Desbordes-Valmore informed the contemporary critic Sainte-Beuve's assertion that "she was born on the side of the people; if she favors the people, it is because she saw in them the distress of those who were banished, massacred, or impoverished. By feeling and by experience, she belonged to the clan of the victims" (qtd. in Bertrand 8). When we read *Sarah*, it is helpful for us to consider her social vulnerability in conjunction with a more detailed look at her proximity, over the course of her voyage, to the turbulent events of the revolutionary Caribbean.

The departure of Catherine and Marceline Desbordes from Bordeaux for Guadeloupe in mid-January 1802 coincided with the arrival in Saint-Domingue (the ultraprofitable French colony that would later become known as Haiti) of a massive French military expedition led by Napoléon's brother-in-law, General Leclerc. Napoléon had sent this army of more than twenty thousand soldiers to wrestle the colony, hovering on the brink of independence, back from the increasing control of its "governor general for life," the former slave Toussaint Louverture (Dayan 149). The revolution in Haiti, which had begun in dialogue with the claims made and debates generated in the French Revolution, both influenced and was influenced by the events of 1802 in Guadeloupe. The closing of Guadeloupe's ports by order of Admiral Lacrosse was a symptom of larger power rivalries and ideological conflicts in the colonial arena. Lacrosse had originally come to Guadeloupe for several months in 1793 with the mission of revolutionizing the island, but he was replaced. He returned to Guadeloupe in 1801, not to revolutionize the island but to repress the revolution, after the famous revolutionary leader Victor Hugues was recalled by the consulate. Lacrosse's attempts to reestablish a harsh colonial program, including the repatriation of exiled colonists and the arrest of many nonwhite military officers, resulted in violent resistance. After being forcibly expelled by officers of color, Lacrosse was then seized by the British, who took him as a prisoner to the British island of Dominica. In Guadeloupe, the Martinican mulatto officer Pélage gained power, stabilized the conflict, and governed successfully.

But France and Britain were in the process of reaching a treaty (the Treaty of Amiens) that would make them allies rather than enemies, and Lacrosse soon found himself not a prisoner but a power broker among France, England, and the Caribbean. He viewed Pélage as a usurper and, with the support of the British navy, barred all ships from landing at Guadeloupe in order to prevent the resumption of normal trade relations with the colony. On 6 May 1802, General Richepanse, with over three thousand men, arrived from France, possibly with the plan of restoring Lacrosse to power. Received cooperatively by Pélage, Richepanse reopened the port shortly thereafter.

It was at this point that Desbordes-Valmore and her mother left Saint-Barthélemy, which, given its status as a neutral zone under its current Swedish ownership, probably served as a place of refuge for colonists fleeing unrest from other colonies, including Saint-Domingue. This time Marceline and Catherine successfully disembarked in Guadeloupe. In the meantime, the Martinican mulatto officer Delgrès, who had been governing with Pélage, split ranks with Pélage and on 10 May instigated a movement of military resistance to Richepanse. Violence raged until 20 May, at which point the ancien régime colonial system was officially restored by the French. Delgrès settled on a dramatic and symbolic resolution: on 28 May, he and hundreds of his followers, cornered by Napoléon's soldiers on the heights of Matouba, used explosives to blow up their attackers as well as themselves. This radical performance of the choice of death over slavery also resulted in some of the most famous stories about women martyrs of the Napoleonic era, including the execution of the wife of Delgrès and of the pregnant "mulâtresse" named Solitude (Schwarz-Bart). The event registered profoundly in the consciousness of fellow revolutionaries in Haiti. In an 1804 proclamation, the former slave leader Jean-Jacques Dessalines commemorated "the brave and immortal Delgresse [Louis Delgrès], who blew himself sky high with the debris of his fort rather than submit to chains" (23).

It is impossible to know specifically which elements of these events Marceline was or was not aware of, either then or later. Ambrière notes that she spoke of the pain of seeing, during the suppression of the slave rebellion, "blacks locked up 'in an iron cage'" (1: 103). But the spectacle of horror that was directly before her eyes was the yellow fever epidemic. Yellow fever would take the life of General Richepanse in September and, in Saint-Domingue, of General Leclerc in November. For Marceline's story, the crucial fact is that Catherine fell ill almost immediately after their arrival in Pointe-à-Pitre in mid-May and perished by late May. Marceline, a teenager without financial or familial support, then had to find a way back to France.

The time line of her journey home reveals her continued close calls with unfolding crises in the history of Western race relations. In early June of 1802, Toussaint Louverture was kidnapped by the French and sent to languish in the Fort de Joux in the Jura. Before Toussaint was transferred from Gonaives to Cap Français, according to Pamphile de Lacroix, he said to the division chief Savary, commander of the vessel, "In overthrowing me, they have only knocked over in Saint-Domingue the trunk of the tree of the liberty of the blacks; it will grow back by the roots, for they are deep and numerous" (203). From Cap Français he sailed to Brest, arriving in mid-July. The British poet William Wordsworth composed the sonnet "To Toussaint Louverture" in August 1802, less than a month after Toussaint's arrival in France, in which he urged "the most unhappy of men" to "take comfort": "There's not a breathing of the common wind / That will forget thee."

On 18 June, Marceline sailed from Pointe-à-Pitre to Basse-Terre. Shortly thereafter, she is thought to have taken another ship to Saint-Domingue. Marceline's journey on the *Eagle*, which left Cap Français on 7 July 1802 and arrived in Brest on 18 August, took place one month after Toussaint Louverture's fateful transatlantic crossing. Back in France, she rebuilt her career as an actress, luridly billed as "a survivor of the disasters on Guadeloupe" (Ambrière 1: 116).

"My Return to Europe," in the first part of her *Huit femmes* ("Eight Women"), presents historical memory as a traumatic construct, peopled by phantoms whose voices the narrator may have poorly retained or poorly translated. These phantoms from the past remained lodged in her memory, indistinctly known but sincerely loved. She asks, "Are we truly certain of what is real when we believe we are writing history?" This question resonates with recent scholarship, such as Christopher Miller's "Forget Haiti," on the fragmentary representation of African diasporan achievements and events in European historiography, making the zone of the revolutionary Caribbean a particularly nebulous field of the real. *Sarah* helps us read the phantoms of the colonial past in French literature.

Readers can best understand Desbordes-Valmore's novella *Sarah* in relation to literary and historical contexts. Antislavery writing in France in the late eighteenth and early nineteenth centuries provides one context. That writing was especially active in the years preceding the emancipation of slaves in 1794, at the height of the French Revolution. Leading abolitionist writers of the time include the marquis de Condorcet, the abbé Raynal, and Henri Grégoire. These and other French antislavery writers were inspired and often directly assisted by such notable English abolitionists as William Wilberforce and Thomas Clarkson.

However, in the aftermath of the revolts in Saint-Domingue and Guadeloupe and Napoléon's revocation of abolition in 1802, there was a general retreat in France from the earlier support for abolition. During the first two decades of the nineteenth century, as Yves Bénot explains in *La démence coloniale sous Napoléon* ("Colonial Delirium in the Napoleonic Era"), proslavery policies prevailed, and there occurred only indirect forms of opposition. The year in which *Sarah* was first published, 1821, marks a renewal of public antislavery activity, with the creation of the Société de la Morale Chrétienne. Created and dominated by Protestants such as Auguste de Staël, the son of Germaine de Staël, and other influential liberals such as her son-in-law, the duc de Broglie, the society was devoted to various charitable causes, including better treatment of slaves and an end to the illegal abduction of slaves from Africa. Desbordes-Valmore is in line with these antislavery positions, at least in *Sarah*, although more generally, as Aimée Boutin observes, "there are too few statements in her correspondence for us to fully understand her position on the abolition of the slave trade" (xxii).

Certain discursive and plot conventions in *Sarah* come into sharper focus when read in relation to French, English, and American women writers from the late seventeenth century to the middle of the nineteenth century—Aphra Behn, Germaine de Staël, Olympe de Gouges, Claire de Duras, George Sand, Harriet Beecher Stowe, and many others—who, like Desbordes-Valmore, link issues of love, marriage, and the family to the condition of slaves. These writers tend to highlight the maternal care and moral agency provided by black and white women. Placing *Sarah* in the context of a larger phenomenon of women's antislavery writing helps counterbalance what scholars like Naomi Schor have criticized as a tendency to undervalue women's idealist writing as minor, feminine, and sentimental (see also Cohen).

Traces of the late-eighteenth and early-nineteenth-century works of Jean-Jacques Rousseau, Jacques-Henri Bernardin de Saint-Pierre, and François-Auguste-René de Chateaubriand are also evident in *Sarah*. For the generation of French Romantic writers of the 1820s, a sentimental or melodramatic style was common, as was the emphasis on the local color afforded by the description of foreign places. Also common were stories about black characters, as Léon-François Hoffmann explains in *Le nègre romantique: Personnage littéraire et obsession collective* ("The Romantic-Era Black: Literary Character and Collective Obsession"). The touching story that Desbordes-Valmore tells of two children raised on an island and bound together by an undying love echoes Bernardin de Saint-Pierre's influential *Paul et Virginie*, a work that stands as the *locus classicus* of French Romantic prose. In Sainte-Beuve's introduction to Desbordes-Valmore's poetry in 1842, he compares the author with Virginie: both are young girls who undertake the perilous voyage from the islands bound for France (Boutin xiv). As late as 1877, Flaubert uses the names Paul and Virginie in "Un cœur simple," in an ironic reference to the lingering effects of Romanticism in the society of his time.

The popularity of the genre of sentimental writing and its relation to abolitionist rhetoric should also be taken into account in contextualizing *Sarah*. In 1821, when Desbordes-Valmore wrote the novella, the cause of antislavery was gaining in popularity and public acceptance. Abolitionist sentiment links the white reader and the enslaved African in the construction of family built on such common building blocks as maternity, paternal authority, filial devotion, romantic love, and family bonds. The problem of identification is paramount in a genre that asks readers to see themselves as African families torn asunder and suffering at the hands of inhuman slave traders. Literary antislavery utilized cultural fears of aristocratic vice and degeneracy. In contrast with her much maligned aristocratic counterpart, the bourgeois woman was rhetorically summoned through sentimental discourse to heed the voice of the heart and to illustrate through her beneficent conduct how essential humanity can transcend social hierarchies. The discourse of feeling encompasses narratives of misfortune that portray the humanity of suffering heroes and heroines. It moves the formerly excluded to center stage. Antislavery topoi such as pitting virtue against villainy and innocence against persecution enabled sentimental fiction to reach a popular audience unreceptive to the Enlightenment discourse of reason and argument. Discussions of race entered less erudite cultural genres such as melodrama and popular fiction to bring readers into the text. Sentimental literature ends with a leveling of social classes:

> One of the structural requirements of the process of sentimentalization is a more or less explicit denial of the importance of social hierarchy. It is where social barriers are transgressed, when some kind of *déclassement* occurs, when a shift down the social ladder takes place, that true sentimental epiphany is provoked. (Denby 96)

The characters in *Sarah* conform well to the model of the sentimental narrative. Arsène stands out as the quintessential member of an excluded class whose humanity is celebrated. He is the one who rescues Sarah, who sacrifices his freedom for hers, who serves as her substitute mother. His humanity transcends social hierarchies. He sets a virtuous example that readers are invited to follow. Although placed on the lowest rung of society, he ascends morally to its summit. In sharp contrast, Silvain functions as a villain. Through his greed and resentment, he introduces misfortune into the peaceful world of the Primrose plantation. He causes harm to Edwin, whose love for Sarah he threatens, and to Mr. Primrose, whose property he steals. Basic to the structure of the novel is the opposition between Arsène and Silvain: an opposition that pits black against white, good against evil, sacrifice against selfishness, African against colonial, devotion against ingratitude. Desbordes-Valmore's use of such oppositions, grounded in the logic of the sentimental narrative, takes on a distinctively antislavery meaning. By attributing to a black man the positive moral and spiritual attributes traditionally reserved for whites and by placing Africa above the degraded colonial world, Desbordes-Valmore uses the sentimental genre to give literary embodiment to abolitionist notions.

The similarity and transferability of Sarah's and Arsène's experiences and feelings are supported by the frame structure of the novella. The first frame is opened in "My Return to Europe," in which the unnamed young narrator recounts how her mother died in Guadeloupe, how the narrator strove to return to Europe, and how she listened to (or may have imagined) stories told to her about natives of the colonies. The first of these stories is the story of Sarah, which constitutes the main section of the book (the other stories are unrelated to *Sarah*). The frame narrator describes herself in a way that clearly points to the real author, as both were in the same place (Pointe-à-Pitre, Guadeloupe), at the same time (1802), and under the same circumstances ("after the revolt and my mourning"). The story of Sarah's adventures is recounted by the frame narrator's companion, a young Creole girl named Eugénie, who inhabits the island of Saint-Barthélemy, where the story is set. A multipartite narrative and authorial pattern is thus set in place. It reaches from the real author through the semiautobiographical frame narrator to the fictional embedded narrator, Eugénie. Inaugurating the novel with this series of young girls, Desbordes-Valmore places authority firmly in feminine hands—as opposed, for example, to *Ourika*, which in a more traditional way invests that narrative authority in a male doctor.

An especially important result of the multipartite narrative structure in *Sarah* is that it prepares the way for the reader to see the central character, Sarah, as an extension of the series of feminine figures in the frame. Sarah's colonial experience and economic disempowerment are thus associated, along the narrative chain, with the author's. In the main section of the novel, another narrative participant emerges: the former slave Arsène, who serves as the narrator of his and Sarah's past lives. The thematic bonds among the frame narrator, Sarah, and Arsène are strong. All three have lost their mothers (as has Silvain, interestingly), and that loss is the primary cause of the alienation and estrangement they suffer. Displaced geographically at a young age, the three are forced to adapt to life among strangers. Their stories place them on or near water: the frame narrator en route to Guadeloupe, Sarah on the boat that brings her to the Primrose plantation, Arsène transported from Africa. The result of these thematic bonds is again that meaning passes along the narrative chain. By this association, all the narrative participants are linked to Arsène's condition as a former slave. Revealingly, the frame narrator compares herself to a black in describing her desire to flee the colonies immediately after her mother's death:

> I would have tried what a little black boy from the house where I was staying wanted to try in order to follow me: I would have thrown myself into the sea, believing, like him, that I would find the strength to swim to France.

In addition to such associations with slavery, anti-slavery positions are developed through and in some cases directly by Arsène. Reflections such as the following, assumed to derive from his status as an eyewitness to the horrors of slavery, present the kind of testimony that abolitionists sought to provide to the public:

> Reminiscences unfurled in his memory and reawakened what remains dormant in the heart: love of the native land, the need for freedom. From high on the lofty mountainside, his eyes settled upon the village below where white inhabitants so intently sought shelter from the sun's ardent rays. His eyes wandered along the seashore where some black man, weighed down by a heavy burden in the burning heat of the day, seemed, like himself, to send a sigh of regret and farewell to his homeland as he succumbed to his fate. He pitied this slave, all slaves.

Emphasizing love of country, the need for freedom, and solidarity with other blacks through their common oppression are important elements in an African perspective on slavery. Associating that perspective with the viewpoints of the frame narrator and Sarah gives added weight and authority to the slave's testimony, just as American slave narratives were typically endorsed and authorized by white sympathizers and sponsors.

That *Sarah* does not locate the primary consciousness of the evils of slavery in white characters is noteworthy. It is Arsène who expresses the main criticisms of slavery in the text and who in fact expresses doubt about the ability of Sarah and Edwin to maintain their innocence once they become adults in a slave-owning society. Arsène's first-hand reflections on this issue contrast sharply with narrative approaches to slavery in texts such as George Sand's *Indiana*. In that novel, the condition of women and the condition of slaves are similarly explored for their analogous experiences of oppression, but the white heroine entirely appropriates the subjectivity and criticism of both women's and slaves' suffering (see Jenson, *Trauma* 183–209). Desbordes-Valmore's narrative in this sense reflects, if only obliquely, her experience of historical moments in the early-nineteenth-century French Caribbean in which blacks were the agents of their own resistance and, in Haiti, the founders of their own postcolonial nation.

Sarah preceded many of what are now the best-known Romantic texts on colonial themes, including Duras's 1823 *Ourika*, Victor Hugo's 1826 novel-length version of *Bug-Jargal*, George Sand's 1832 *Indiana*, and Alphonse de Lamartine's 1850 *Toussaint Louverture*. A precursor of sorts, it deserves notice also as a fictional condensation of the orphaned author's experience of black revolutionary history into an epiphany of maternal recognition between a white female heroine and a male former slave.

When Sarah, after listening to Arsène's descriptions of an African mother's all-suffering devotion, cries, "Then I will call you my mother, . . . because you have done all that for me!," she is forging a new pathway of interracial recognition and identification. Early in French Romanticism, Desbordes-Valmore thus both borrows from and exceeds existing models of emancipation in sentimental literature. Likewise, if in abolitionism the question was to have slavery or not have slavery, in *Sarah* this question is nuanced to include the problem of how to recognize and prevent enslavement and reenslavement—a question that remains highly relevant to our readings of social hierarchies and their histories today.

Notes

[1] Unless otherwise indicated, all translations in this introduction are ours.

[2] For the relation of these poems to early Creole poetry, see Jenson, "Polyphonie."

[3] That she used her real names—either her family name, Desbordes; her husband's name, Valmore; or the two combined, but not placing the husband's name first, as was the custom—indicates that, unlike many women writers in early-nineteenth-century France, she felt free to operate as a woman in the public arena. She negotiated the contract of her first book, *Elégies, Marie et romances*, in 1818, independently of her husband's control, although she had him countersign the contract as a token of his conjugal authority.

[4] The critique of the vulnerability and subjugation of women in *Sarah* may seem to be undermined by frequent praise of Sarah's humility and submission. But in the early decades of the nineteenth century, virtually any writing by French women functioned as an act of autonomy and thus of liberation from patriarchal control. As James Smith Allen has observed, the failure to address women's rights explicitly should not obscure the fact that these women developed a language that expressed women's historical identity, agency, and resistance (171).

Works Cited

Allen, James Smith. *Poignant Relations: Three Modern Women.* Baltimore: Johns Hopkins UP, 2000.

Ambrière, Francis. *Le siècle des Valmore: Marceline Desbordes-Valmore et les siens.* 2 vols. Paris: Seuil, 1987.

Bénot, Yves. *La démence coloniale sous Napoléon.* Paris: La Découverte, 1992.

Bertrand, Marc. Introduction. Desbordes-Valmore *Œuvres* 1: 5–10.

Boutin, Aimée. *Maternal Echoes: The Poetry of Marceline Desbordes-Valmore and Alphonse de Lamartine.* Delaware: Delaware UP, 2001.

Cohen, Margaret. *The Sentimental Education of the Novel.* Princeton: Princeton UP, 1999.

Dayan, Joan. *Haiti, History, and the Gods.* Berkeley: U of California P, 1995.

Denby, David J. *Sentimental Narrative and the Social Order in France, 1760–1820.* Cambridge: Cambridge UP, 1994.

Desbordes-Valmore, Marceline. *Les œuvres poétiques de Marceline Desbordes-Valmore.* Ed. Marc Bertrand. 2 vols. Grenoble: PU de Grenoble, 1973.

Dessalines, Jean-Jacques. "Liberté ou la mort: N. 13: Proclamation relative au massacre des français." *Recueil général des lois et actes du gouvernement d' Haïti.* Ed. S. Linstant de Pradine. Paris: Durand, 1886. 21–25.

Dubois, Laurent. *A Colony of Citizens: Revolution and Slave Emancipation in the French Caribbean, 1787–1804.* Chapel Hill: U of North Carolina P, 2004.

Flaubert, Gustave. "Un cœur simple." *Trois contes.* Project Gutenberg. 1 Apr. 2004. 10 Dec. 2007 <http://www.gutenberg.org/etext/12065>.

Hoffmann, Léon-François. *Le nègre romantique: Personnage littéraire et obsession collective.* Paris: Payot, 1973.

Jenson, Deborah. "Polyphonie sociale dans la poésie créole de Saint-Domingue (Haïti)." *Langue et identité narrative dans les littératures de l'ailleurs.* Ed. Marie-Christine Hazaël-Massieux and Michel Bertrand. Aix-en-Provence: PU de Provence, 2005. 171–96.

———. *Trauma and Its Representations: The Social Life of Mimesis in Post-revolutionary France*. Baltimore: Johns Hopkins UP, 2001.

Lacroix, Pamphile de. *Mémoires pour servir à l'histoire de Saint-Domingue*. Paris: Pillet, 1819.

Miller, Christopher. "Forget Haiti: Baron Roger and the New Africa." *The Haiti Issue: 1804 and Nineteenth-Century French Studies*. Ed. Deborah Jenson. Spec. issue of *Yale French Studies* 107 (2005): 39–69.

Sand, George. *Indiana*. Paris: Gallimard, 1984.

Schor, Naomi. *Breaking the Chain: Women, Theory, and French Realist Fiction*. New York: Columbia UP, 1985.

Schwarz-Bart, André. *La mûlatresse Solitude*. Paris: Seuil, 1972.

Wordsworth, William. "To Toussaint Louverture." *Poems, in Two Volumes, and Other Poems, 1800–1807*. Ed. Jared Curtis. Ithaca: Cornell UP, 1983. 160–61.

SELECTED WORKS BY MARCELINE DESBORDES-VALMORE

Major Works

Elégies, Marie et romances. Paris: Louis, 1819.

Poésies. Paris: Louis, 1820.

Les veillées des Antilles. Paris: Louis, 1821.

Poésies de Madame Desbordes-Valmore. Paris: Grandin, 1822.

Elégies et poésies nouvelles. Paris: Ladvocat, 1825.

A mes jeunes amis: Album du jeune âge. Paris: Boulland, 1830.

L'atelier d'un peintre: Scènes de la vie privée. Paris: Charpentier, 1833.

Les pleurs: Poésies nouvelles. Paris: Charpentier, 1833.

Une raillerie de l'amour. Paris: Charpentier, 1833.

Le salon de Lady Betty: Mœurs anglaises. Paris: Charpentier, 1836.

Pauvres fleurs. Paris: Dumont, 1839.

Violette. Paris: Dumont, 1839.

Le livre des mères et des enfants: Contes et vers en prose. Lyon: Boitel, 1840.

Bouquets et prières. Paris: Dumont, 1843.

Huit femmes. Paris: Chlendowski, 1845.

Les anges de la famille. Paris: Desesserts, 1849.

Jeunes têtes et jeunes cœurs. Paris: Bonneville, 1855.

Posthumous Works

Poésies inédites. Genève: Fick, 1860.

Œuvres poétiques. 3 vols. Paris: Lemerre, 1886.

Correspondance intime. Ed. Benjamin Rivière. 2 vols. Paris: Lemerre, 1896.

Recent Editions

Les œuvres poétiques de Marceline Desbordes-Valmore. Ed. Marc Bertrand. 2 vols. Grenoble: PU de Grenoble, 1973.

Poésies. Ed. Yves Bonnefoy. Paris: Gallimard, 1983.

Contes. Ed. Marc Bertrand. Lyon: PU de Lyon, 1989.

Les petits flamands. Ed. Marc Bertrand. Genève: Droz, 1991.

L'atelier d'un peintre: Scènes de la vie privée: Roman. Ed. Georges Dottin. Calais: Miroirs, 1992.

Domenica. Ed. Marc Bertrand. Genève: Droz, 1992.

Huit femmes. Ed. Marc Bertrand. Genève: Droz, 1999.

Les veillées des Antilles. Ed. Aimée Boutin. Paris: L'Harmattan, 2006.

SUGGESTIONS FOR FURTHER READING

Critical and Biographical Studies of Marceline Desbordes-Valmore

Ambrière, Francis. *Le siècle des Valmore: Marceline Desbordes-Valmore et les siens*. 2 vols. Paris: Seuil, 1987.

Baudelaire, Charles. "Réflexions sur quelques-uns de mes contemporains." *Œuvres complètes*. Ed. Y.-G. Le Dantec and Claude Pichois. Paris: Gallimard, 1961.

Béaunier, André. *Visages de femmes*. Paris: Plon-Nourrit, 1913.

Bertrand, Marc. *Une femme à l'écoute de son temps: Marceline Desbordes-Valmore*. Lyon: La Cigogne, 1997.

Bertrand-Jennings, Chantal. *Un autre mal du siècle: Le romantisme des romancières*. Toulouse: PU du Mirail, 2005.

Bivort, Olivier. "Les 'Vies absentes' de Rimbaud et de Marceline Desbordes-Valmore." *Revue d'histoire littéraire de la France* 101 (2001): 1269–73.

Boulenger, Jacques. *Desbordes-Valmore d'après ses papiers inédits*. Paris: Fayard, 1909.

Boutin, Aimée. "Colonial Memory, Narrative, and Sentimentalism in Desbordes-Valmore's *Les Veillées des Antilles*." Paliyenko, *Gender* 57–67.

———. *Maternal Echoes: The Poetry of Marceline Desbordes-Valmore and Alphonse de Lamartine*. Newark: Delaware UP, 2001.

Danahy, Michael. "1859: Marceline Desbordes-Valmore." Hollier 731–37.

———. "Marceline Desbordes-Valmore and the Engendered Canon." *Yale French Studies* 75 (1988):129–47.

Descaves, Lucien. *La vie douleureuse de Marceline Desbordes-Valmore.* Paris: Nilsson, 1910.

Ferguson, Simone D. "Marceline Desbordes-Valmore: Une voix féminine au milieu du carnage des révolutions." *Revue francophone de Louisiane* 6.2 (1991): 27–35.

———. "Woman as Creator: Marceline Desbordes-Valmore's Transformation of the Lyric." *Nineteenth Century French Studies* 21.1–2 (1992–1993): 57–65.

Greenberg, Wendy. *Uncanonical Women: Feminine Voice in French Poetry, 1830–1871.* Amsterdam: Rodopi, 1999.

Hollier, Denis, ed. *A New History of French Literature.* Cambridge: Harvard UP, 1989.

Jasenas, Eliane. *Marceline Desbordes-Valmore devant la critique.* Geneva: Droz, 1962.

Jenson, Deborah. "Myth, History, and Witnessing in Marceline Desbordes-Valmore's Caribbean Poetics." Paliyenko, *Gender* 81–92.

———. "Polyphonie sociale dans la poésie créole de Saint-Domingue (Haïti)." *Langue et identité narrative dans les littératures de l'ailleurs.* Ed. Marie-Christine Hazaël-Massieux and Michel Bertrand. Aix-en-Provence: PU de Provence, 2005. 171–96.

———. *Trauma and Its Representations: The Social Life of Mimesis in Post-revolutionary France.* Baltimore: Johns Hopkins UP, 2001.

Johnson, Barbara. "1820: The Lady in the Lake." Hollier 627–31.

———. "1859: Marceline Desbordes-Valmore." Hollier 731–37.

———. "Gender and Poetry: Charles Baudelaire and Marceline Desbordes-Valmore." *The Feminist Difference:*

Literature, Psychoanalysis, Race, and Gender. Cambridge: Harvard UP, 1998. 101–28.

Kadish, Doris. "'Sarah' and Antislavery." Paliyenko, *Gender* 93–104.

Kaplan, Edward K. "The Voices of Marceline Desbordes-Valmore: Deference, Self-Assertion, Accountability." *French Forum* 22.3 (1997): 261–77.

Lloyd, Rosemary. "Baudelaire, Marceline Desbordes-Valmore et la fraternité des poètes." *Bulletin Baudelairien* 26.2 (1991): 65–74.

McCall, Anne E. "Monuments of the Maternal: Reflections on the Desbordes-Valmore Correspondence." *Esprit Créateur* 39.2 (1999): 41–51.

Paliyenko, Adrianna M., ed. *Gender and Race: Romantic-Era Women and French Colonial Memory*. Spec. ed. of *L'Esprit Créateur* 47.4 (2007): 1–134.

———. "(Re)Placing Women in French Poetic History: The Romantic Legacy." *Symposium: A Quarterly Journal in Modern Literatures* 53.4 (2000): 261–82.

———. "Returns of Marceline Desbordes-Valmore's Repressed Memory." Paliyenko, *Gender* 68–80.

Planté, Christine. "L'art sans art de Marceline Desbordes-Valmore." *Europe: Revue littéraire mensuelle* May 1987: 164–75.

———. "*L'atelier d'un peintre* de Marceline Desbordes-Valmore: Le roman d'une poète." *George Sand Studies* 17.1–2 (1998): 43–54.

———. "'J'en étais': Le je du poète et la communauté chez Marceline Desbordes-Valmore." *Le moi, l'histoire, 1789–1848*. Ed. Chantal Mossol. Grenoble: ELLUG, 2005. 117–32.

———. "Marceline Desbordes-Valmore: L'autobiographie indéfinie." *Romantisme: Revue du dix-neuvième siècle* 17.56 (1987): 48–58.

———. "Marceline Desbordes-Valmore: Ni poésie feminine, ni poésie féministe." *French Literature Series* 16 (1989): 78–93.

Porter, Laurence M. "Poetess or Strong Poet? Gender Stereotypes and the Elegies of Marceline Desbordes-Valmore." *French Forum* 18.2 (1993): 185–94.

Pougin, Arthur. *La jeunesse de Marceline Desbordes-Valmore.* Paris: Lévy, 1898.

Sainte-Beuve, Charles Augustin. *Portraits contemporains.* Paris: Didier, 1855.

Schultz, Gretchen. "Gender and the Sonnet: Marceline Desbordes-Valmore and Paul Verlaine." *Cincinnati Romance Review* 10 (1991): 190–99.

Verlaine, Paul. *Les poètes maudits.* Ed. Michel Décaudin. Paris: SEDES, 1982.

Selected Works on the Revolutionary Caribbean, Abolitionism, Sentimentalism, and Colonial-Themed French Literature

Allen, James Smith. *Poignant Relations: Three Modern Women.* Baltimore: Johns Hopkins UP, 2000.

Aravamudan, Srinivas. *Tropicopolitans: Colonialism and Agency, 1688–1804.* Durham: Duke UP, 1999.

Bongie, Chris. *Islands and Exiles: The Creole Identities of Post/colonial Literature.* Stanford: Stanford UP, 1998.

Cohen, Margaret. *The Sentimental Education of the Novel.* Princeton: Princeton UP, 1999.

Cohen, William B. *The French Encounter with Africans: White Response to Blacks, 1530–1880.* Bloomington: Indiana UP, 1980.

Denby, David J. *Sentimental Narrative and the Social Order in France, 1760–1820.* Cambridge: Cambridge UP, 1994.

Descourtilz, Michel-Etienne. *Voyages d'un naturaliste.* 3 vols. Paris: Dufart, 1809.

Dubois, Laurent. *A Colony of Citizens: Revolution and Slave Emancipation in the French Caribbean, 1787–1804.* Chapel Hill: U of North Carolina P, 2004.

Dubois, Laurent, and John D. Garrigus. *Slave Revolution in the Caribbean, 1789–1804: A Brief History with Documents*. New York: Palgrave-Macmillan, 2006.

Fouchard, Jean. *Le théâtre à Saint-Domingue*. Port-au-Prince: Deschamps, 1988.

Garraway, Doris. *The Libertine Colony: Creolization in the Early French Caribbean*. Durham: Duke UP, 2005.

Gaspar, David Barry, and David P. Geggus. *A Turbulent Time: The French Revolution and the Greater Caribbean*. Bloomington: Indiana UP, 1997.

Haudrère, Philippe, and Françoise Vergès. *De l'esclave au citoyen*. Paris: Gallimard, 1998.

Hoffmann, Léon-François. *Le nègre romantique: Personnage littéraire et obsession collective*. Paris: Payot, 1973.

James, C. L. R. *The Black Jacobins: Toussaint L'Ouverture and the San Domingo Revolution*. London: Secker, 1938.

Jenson, Deborah, ed. *The Haiti Issue: 1804 and Nineteenth-Century French Studies*. Spec. issue of *Yale French Studies* 107 (2005): 1–188.

Kadish, Doris, ed. *Slavery in the Francophone Caribbean World: Distant Voices, Forgotten Acts, Forged Identities*. Athens: U of Georgia P, 2000.

Kadish, Doris Y., and Françoise Massardier-Kenney. *Translating Slavery: Gender and Race in French Women's Writing, 1783–1823*. Kent: Kent State UP, 1994.

Lacour, Auguste. *Histoire de la Guadeloupe*. Aubenas, Fr.: Habauzit, 1960.

Lacroix, Pamphile de. *Mémoires pour servir à l'histoire de Saint-Domingue*. Paris: Pillet, 1819.

Linstant de Pradine, S., ed. *Recueil général des lois et des actes du Gouvernement d'Haïti, 1804–1808*. Paris: Durand; Pédone-Lauriel, 1886.

Miller, Christopher L. *Blank Darkness: Africanist Discourse in French*. Chicago: Chicago UP, 1985.

Peabody, Sue. *There Are No Slaves in France: The Political Culture of Race and Slavery in the Ancien Régime.* New York: Oxford UP, 1996.

Sala-Molins, Louis. *Le code noir, ou, le calvaire de Canaan.* Paris: PU de France, 1987.

Schor, Naomi. *Breaking the Chain: Women, Theory, and French Realist Fiction.* New York: Columbia UP, 1985.

Trouillot, Michel-Rolph. *Silencing the Past: Power and the Production of History.* Boston: Beacon, 1995.

William Wordsworth. "To Toussaint Louverture." *Poems, in Two Volumes, and Other Poems, 1800–1807.* Ed. Jared Curtis. Ithaca: Cornell UP, 1983. 160–61.

TRANSLATORS' NOTE

In our translation of *Sarah*, we sought to be faithful to the words and sentences of Desbordes-Valmore's text and thus to achieve, as much as possible, semantic and syntactic equivalence (Bassnett-McGuire 27, 56). Accordingly, we decided to render the poem that the novella contains in a free, relatively literal translation rather than rhymed verse. We also tried to make only minimal changes to sentences. We reduced the number of short phrases to make the text easier to read but in ways that did not affect its meaning or tone. For example, "Les femmes créoles ne savent pas courir; mais leur taille élégante et souple se déploie avec une simplicité noble; on les suit du cœur" becomes "Creole women do not know how to run. But their supple, elegant figures move forward with a noble simplicity that touches the heart." In some cases, small changes were made for the sake of consistency: for example, the name "Silvain" appears as both "Silvain" and "Sylvain" in the original.

Along with semantic and syntactic equivalence, we attempted pragmatically to capture the strong emotions that Desbordes-Valmore's text aims to elicit in readers. To evoke the sentimental tone of the text as a whole, we raised the register of the language at times, using diction that characterizes eighteenth-century and early-nineteenth-century sentimental literature in English: "perish" for *mourir*, "retreat" for *s'en aller*, "weep" for *pleurer*. Antislavery works published in Britain in the late eighteenth century provide parallel texts or models in English for many of Desbordes-Valmore's stock phrases, exclamations, and terms of endearment. An example can be drawn from Maria Edgeworth's "The Grateful Negro": "Kindness was new to him; it overpowered his manly heart; and at hearing the words 'my good friend,' the tears gushed from his eyes: tears which no torture could have extorted!" (405). Although we do not use exactly the same expressions, our solutions at times approximate the emotional, antislavery tone of Edgeworth's writing. We are also attentive, however, to a modern sense of undecidability in Desbordes-Valmore's poetic writing, even in passages dominated by the sentimental rhetoric of the era (Planté 46–47).

The representation of orality is an important philosophical element of *Sarah*, which includes not only women's and children's stories but also stories told by slaves. The association of orality with African diasporan cultural survival has been made by numerous critics (Kadish and Massardier-Kenney 23), and *Sarah* exemplifies this association through two particular idiosyncratic techniques in addition to the use of narrative frames. When the slave Arsène tells his story or that of Sarah's mother, paragraph structure essentially disappears, a marker of orality that we chose to preserve. With quotation marks and dashes we also tried to reflect Desbordes-Valmore's unusual practice of using a left guillemet to indicate the oral nature of the story, followed by a dash to indicate direct speech within the story, for its thematic value.

Part of the oral quality of *Sarah* is a breathless, emotional style, and there are occasional passages where the logic of the narration is not entirely clear. In such passages we chose to modify slightly the original text, in rare cases adding minor elements for the purpose of clarification. To give one example:

> One evening, when the air was as still as it is today, when nothing troubled the calm of the shore, and the sea was as blue and harmonious as the sky, Edwin Primrose, a child of our island, stood beyond the gate that you can see from here.

In the original, he appears "devant la porte" (literally, "before the door"), which could be either inside or outside the house. By placing him "beyond the gate," we try to specify a position that enables him to see the coastline. Another, especially confusing example occurs in a passage that describes the disturbed sleep of various members of the plantation household one night:

> Edwin croyant lire encore auprès de Sarah, lui donnait mille fois les noms que recelait son livre. Sarah les écoutait en silence, et les cachait dans son âme comme un présent d'Edwin. Ces noms troublaient son sommeil, mais ils l'enchantaient.

A close English translation would read:

> Edwin, believing he was still reading near Sarah, attributed to her a thousand times the names contained in his book.

Sarah listened to them in silence, and hid them in her soul as a gift from Edwin. These names disturbed her sleep, but they also enchanted her.

Since Edwin's sleep and their location in separate bedrooms makes literal dialogue impossible, the translation contains the following modification of the original text:

Edwin dreamed that he was still reading next to Sarah, and in his sleep he offered her a thousand times the precious names concealed in his book. Sarah listened in silence, and stowed his words away in her soul as a precious gift. These names then troubled but also enchanted her sleep.

A major decision concerned the translation of the words *nègre* and *noir* in the original.[1] Our basic premise, based on historical research into the use of such terms, is that "black" avoids the pejorative connotations that *nègre* and *Negro* have had and continue in some cases to have today (Kadish and Massardier-Kenney 18–20). At the time of *Sarah*'s publication, *nègre* connoted slave, whereas *noir* had become associated with abolitionist politics. Where *nègre* clearly connotes slavery in French, we translated it as "slave." In most cases, the word is translated as "black" or "black man"; in a few cases, where it adds nothing to the meaning of the text, it is dropped altogether. Overall, in matters regarding the linguistic markers of race, where no one rendering attains the ideal of simultaneous cultural precision and freedom from restrictive cultural typologies, we attempted to conform to standard modern practice.

Note

[1] We retained the lower case for nouns of color (black and white), which is found in the original, as opposed to the upper case, which appears in the Bertrand edition.

Works Cited

Bassnett-McGuire, Susan. *Translation Studies*. London: Methuen, 1980.

Edgeworth, Maria. "The Grateful Negro." *Popular Tales*. New York: AMS, 1967. 399–420. Vol. 2 of *Tales and Novels*.

Kadish, Doris Y., and Françoise Massardier-Kenney. *Translating Slavery: Gender and Race in French Women's Writing, 1783–1823*. Kent: Kent State UP, 1994.

Planté, Christine. "*L'atelier d'un peintre* de Marceline Desbordes-Valmore: Le roman d'une poète." *George Sand Studies* 17.1–2 (1998): 43–54.

MARCELINE DESBORDES-VALMORE

Sarah

My Return to Europe

Yellow fever continued to ravage Pointe-à-Pitre, but there was nothing more it could take from me. I was soon to reembark alone on a ship in the harbor that would then anchor in Basse-Terre to add to its cargo before setting sail for France.

Night had already fallen, with the palpable darkness that alters the look of places, inventing new cities in the place of those seen by day. Unable to bear the sight of the city thus transformed, I fled to a low back room in the house where I had sought refuge since the slave revolt and my mother's death. Listening to the seconds tick by, waiting for the old clock against the wall to strike the hour of my departure, I was visited by the Governor, who came on behalf of his wife to offer me refuge with his family, until I could return to France at a less perilous time. He informed the widow with whom I had lodged of the dangers that awaited me on this ship, so frail that it resembled little more than a large covered barge.

This commercial boat, bringing salt cod, whale oil, and other products to Brest, carried no provisions other than a few pieces of dried beef and hardtack to be divided up with a hammer. The fires in the ship's binnacle and the sailors' pipes were the only ones that would be lit to warm the long voyage.

"She will perish," said the Governor to the young widow who already mourned my fate. "Upon my word, Madame, she will perish."

I heard every word they said through the thin wall, but nothing changed my determination to leave. They came to gain my assent to their plans. I wept, but refused their offers, horrified at the prospect of staying there. It seemed to me that, rather than stay, I would have tried what a black boy from the house wanted to do in order to accompany me: throw myself in the sea, believing, as he did, that my arms would find the strength to transport me to France.

Terror chased me from this moving island. An earthquake a few days earlier had thrown me onto the bed while I was standing before a little mirror, braiding my hair. I feared the walls, the sounds of the leaves, the air. The cries of the birds made me want to leave. In this whole population, dying or in mourning for the dead, the birds alone seemed alive to me, because they had wings. The Governor received no more for his troubles than my gratitude and a farewell. I can still see his desolate expression as he went out, abandoning me to my destiny, which he feared would be fatal. It was the first time that I made up my own mind, trusting myself to God alone, now my only master.

At midnight I departed. The widow, who escorted me to the ship, could not bring herself to take leave of me when the time came. Without telling me, she sent her most trusted servants back to the house, and resolved to accompany me the full forty-five leagues separating the two islands.

When we reached the harbor and I felt myself being led away by sailors from the ship, I put my hand over my eyes, unable to bear the sight of this kind woman's tears. Imagine my surprise at finding her next to me in the launch, calm and satisfied as when a conflict is generously resolved. She accompanied me to Basse-Terre, where she had friends, hoping against hope to find a better passage for me to Europe in the days before the ship set sail. She wrapped her arms around me, and we no longer spoke a word as we took in the spectacle that surrounded us.

On one side, the ocean stretched out in an immense surface, black and shining, the moon's reflection prismatically reproduced with each fleeting wave. I turned back to gaze upon the receding port, which was hardly recognizable as the one at which I had arrived earlier, during a storm. Its silent activity was revealed only in the movement of lights from boat to boat. In the midst of these sights, which have remained etched in my mind, I thought I saw my mother running to the bank, holding out her arms, alive again, to me . . . My God! I have had this dream so many times! . . . No memory casts down my spirits like this one. What followed afterward, when I returned to accomplish my destiny in France, that country I so sorely missed but which did not miss me, is of little import compared to this memory. My love of my native land, conceived in the cradle,[1] remains sweet and sadly mysterious, like all loves!

Later, beset during the long crossing by an ardent sun one moment and cold fog the next, I could do nothing but listen to the voices of the new phantoms that passed before my eyes. Were they real or imaginary? Who knows? It is they whom I now fondly evoke, altered, transformed in the slumber of my memory. Housed among my recollections before they were well known, they are still loved there. Do we truly know better those who narrate their stories directly to us, those with whom we live, for whom we suffer, and who suffer for us, than those we merely remember? Are we truly certain of what is real when we believe we are writing history? I beg forgiveness from the narrators whose stories I have remembered poorly, whose words I have ill translated. If

---

[1] The original, "amour du berceau," can connote both love of the native land and love of the mother, whose memory is evoked here.

a few touching lines from all the pages that follow should correspond to the memories of those passengers from long ago, may they receive them as restitution. As for the rest of what follows, pale and languishing as it is, like the dead calm that we suffered through together when it cradled our ship without moving it forward, I alone deserve the blame.

A Young Creole

In Saint-Barthélemy, a politically neutral zone of the Antilles, I saw a lofty mountain whose summit formed an immense plateau on which trees had been planted in even rows. Scattered high on the gentle slope leading to the city are a few charming plantations. The variegated shrubs that grow on this ardent soil intertwine to form a long chain, a unique verdant barrier that conceals the rapid ascent of the terrain and yields a sense of the sublime when, having reached the summit, one contemplates how steep the hill has been.

The viewer is left breathless at the sight of the majestic expanse of the sea. The rocks that swell from its breast seem to part respectfully to allow free passage to the

---

In the first part of the nineteenth century, *Creole* designated a person born in the colonies, whether of European or African descent; it had no stable color connotations. Thus Sarah and Edwin are Creoles, like the narrator Eugénie; Arsène and Mr. Primrose are not. Eugénie, the "young Creole" referred to here, is presumably white.

waves. From this distance, the ships on its surface seem mere birds poised between sea and clouds. The city itself seems a mere hamlet in a deep valley; its scattered red and green low houses look like flowerbeds set in a vast lawn.

Once a cool breeze announces the setting of the sun, one can dare venture forth into air that shimmered with heat earlier in the day. At a languid pace, Creoles set out for the mountainside, the preferred promenade of this sparse population.

The fashionable women of the island seem unfamiliar with French styles and eschew veils of rich lace. In their place, simple madras headdresses seem to float upon their gently bowed and graceful heads.

It is said that French women walk at a run. Like birds, they seem to touch the gravel disdainfully with their delicate feet, a hurried flock that never collides. Looking from afar at this airy swarm making its way through the streets of Paris, one is astonished that they never rise above the ground, which they barely seem to touch.

Creole women do not know how to run. But their supple, elegant figures move forward with a noble simplicity that touches the heart. In their solitary promenades, they sway like the palm trees of their land, with a slight rocking that calms their steady, dreamy gait.

Their soft accent and the tender terms with which they innocently address strangers are a balm to the souls of those who miss their homeland. I missed mine, and I felt the charm of their speech. I experienced their curiosity as benevolence rather than the boldness that can wound those who suffer.

One of these young women, a neighbor who assiduously sought me out, came each day to teach me a few words of her gentle language, which I tried to repeat to the others to honor her efforts. If I made mistakes, they all laughed at me openly, eschewing that fake silence that only mortifies those who recognize its message. A pretty mouth becomes ugly when smiles are deformed by mockery, when features are distorted by attempts to reveal and conceal at the same time. Such constraint was foreign to my young friends. As they burst into charming laughter, I laughed with them. They quarreled over the pleasure of teaching me.

One day our little group, weary of talking and singing during our mountain walks, divided into pairs. Each girl took the arm of her dearest friend. Even innocent hearts have secrets and seek a welcoming repository for their feelings of fear or wonder. My inclination bound me to Eugénie. We were both fourteen years old; and her name, which was also my sister's, inspired my trust.

For a few moments, our conversation was as lively as the games we had been playing. But gradually, shadows settled over the hillside, and the monotonous sound of the waves below darkened our mood. Eugénie could see that my thoughts were elsewhere. Fearing that she too would fall under the sad spell of my estrangement from home, she tried to distract me.

It is true that, although I hardly realized it at the time, a vague fear now cast a shadow over the long and dangerous path stretched out before me: the same path that earlier, protected by a mother's smile, I had traveled without worry or concern. The idea of having to cross the sea alone to see my father once again weighed heavily upon me and brought the carefree days of my childhood to an end. Eugénie could see the distress in the constant redirection of my gaze toward the sea. Never will I forget the innocent ruse she used to capture my attention.

"Look at that plantation on the mountainside," she said. "Whenever I walk that way, it reminds me of Sarah's story. If I had your full attention, I would tell you that story."

I looked at Eugénie with a smile. Then she took my hands in hers, as if entwining our thoughts together, and began her tale.

The Canoe

"One evening, when the air was as still as it is today, when nothing troubled the calm of the shore, and the sea was as blue and harmonious as the sky, Edwin Primrose, a child of our island, stood beyond the gate that you can see from here. While his father read in the shade of the green palms, Edwin busied himself by looking in the distance for some object to nourish his curiosity. Convinced that something was finally approaching, he stared until he discerned a dugout canoe born along softly by the sea. Rowing effortlessly, a black man was traveling in this hollowed tree, in which a child slept peacefully. Edwin, who dared not utter a word for fear of disturbing his father, silently greeted the canoe with outstretched arms, beckoning it with exuberant gestures to approach. The black man, who perceived his presence, gazed upon him warily for some time. Finally yielding to the child's silent invitation, he rowed toward him. Soon he reached the foot of the rocky coast. He carefully lifted the still slumbering little Sarah and, having laid her on a cushion of sea moss, pulled his light canoe ashore to prevent the waves from carrying it away. Then, carrying the sleeping child from her mossy bed, he began to climb the mountainside and soon arrived at the plantation to which Providence seemed to have guided his steps.

"Consumed with curiosity, the white boy anxiously followed the black man's every move. When he bent forward after stumbling on a stone, so too did the boy. When the black man reached level ground, a few steps from him, Edwin put one hand to his lips in a gesture of silence and raised the other in a sign of victory. His father, who had been watching him while pretending to read, awaited the conclusion of this adventure with considerable interest.

11

"He saw his son tiptoe forward and gently touch Sarah, who awoke and smiled back at him. It was as if two angels were meeting on earth and greeting each other with joy.

"The black traveler, serious and thoughtful, seemed lost in profound meditation. Suddenly the silent scene was interrupted by Edwin, who loudly implored:

"— Look! Look, father! Give me this beautiful little child, give me this kind black man who has brought her to me. I want them. Oh father, it is my wish that they stay here forever!

"Impatiently he ran to the child, tried to lift her in his arms, and then jumped on his father's lap. Mr. Primrose embraced him warmly and gestured to the black man to approach.

"— Slave, who is your master? he asked him.

"— I am free, the black man said sadly. And he pulled from his pocket the papers attesting to his emancipation.

"Mr. Primrose read them carefully. The pensive attitude of the black man and the whiteness of the girl in his arms astonished and touched him.

"— Where were you going? he asked.

"— To sell myself, answered the free black man. The price of my freedom will feed little Sarah, who has never known her father and who was left to poor Arsène by her dying mother. I am Arsène. I seek a refuge for her and a master for myself.

"The tears welling up in his eyes touched Mr. Primrose's sympathetic nature. Even little Edwin was brought to tears and stood, with hands clasped, unable to speak.

"— Dry your tears, my son, his father said. You know that your happiness is my pleasure. Black man, you need seek no further for this child's refuge. I welcome you both. She will grow up under your eyes. Join the ranks of my servants; I do not call them my slaves; I need to be loved by them.

"Arsène bowed in gratitude. His feelings were expressed in his eyes, not in the confused words that he stammered in his joy. With expressions of delight, little Edwin clamored around Sarah like a fawn on a grassy slope.

"Mr. Primrose summoned Silvain, the overseer of the plantation, and delivered Arsène to him after briefly communicating his instructions. Silvain listened silently, looking to see whether the black man was young and strong. Arsène was indeed at the peak of youthful vigor. Silvain, after this evaluation, did not blame his master for being overly charitable. And Sarah's childish graces almost brought a smile to the slave keeper's somber visage.

"Thus it was that the orphaned Sarah came to reside in the home of the richest Englishman of our colony. Without understanding her debt to him, she soon repaid it in hundreds of clever ways that enlivened the lonely life of the father and the childhood games of the son, whose

13

young interests and education she shared. Considerably less noisy and distracted than Edwin, she listened carefully to the lessons Mr. Primrose reveled in providing, as teaching distracted him from the grief and boredom that had followed the recent death of his young and beloved wife. His son, who alone made his desolate life bearable, received every attention that Mr. Primrose could spare from his solitary chagrin, from his regret for happiness lost, and from his impatience to rejoin his adored Jenny in the hereafter. He had written his melancholy thoughts on his wife's tomb, which was situated on a small island entirely dedicated to such monuments, whose shore you could see from here.

"The downcast spirits of the English planter, indifferent to his fortune and vast properties, had for some time left him vulnerable to Silvain's mercenary ambitions.

"Silvain represented him everywhere. And as is often the case with servants vested with the authority of their masters, he became wealthy and inspired fear in those who pitied and cherished his master.

"Arsène immediately bore the brunt of this authority, which Silvain barbarously abused, and which the slaves, fearful of his power, dared not reveal. First Silvain asked Arsène for the secret of Sarah's birth; then he demanded it. Shocked by Arsène's refusal, he threatened to obtain by force a secret that he assumed his master possessed and that thus provoked his jealousy and ambition. This secret possessed by his master alone seemed to him a treasure that he ardently desired to acquire. The black man's firm resistance stung Silvain's pride and spurred him on to acts of harsh punishment to exact vengeance. Arsène refrained from all complaint. But he felt himself to be a slave, despite the promises and kindnesses that Mr. Primrose had proffered. Nevertheless, the hope of having acquired a protector for Sarah sustained him in his voluntary captivity. When he gazed upon her in the distance, running freely with Edwin, he took heart, despite the sad thoughts to which the condition of servitude gives rise. Their games, their youth, the joys of innocent gaiety that even cruel Silvain did not dare disrupt, were his only reward. Often overcome by fatigue and heat, Arsène would withdraw from his companions to breathe for a moment, to dare to think of himself, of the parents he had barely known, of the arid but free shores from which white men—men!—deaf to his cries and tears, had torn him away more than twenty years ago. Reminiscences rose up in his mind and reawakened what remains dormant in all men's hearts: love of the native land, the need for freedom. From high on the lofty mountainside, his eyes settled upon the village below, where white inhabitants so intently sought shelter from the sun's ardent rays. His eyes wandered along the seashore, where some black man, weighed down by a heavy burden in the burning

15

heat of the day, seemed, like himself, to send a sigh of regret and farewell to his homeland as he succumbed to his fate. He pitied this slave, all slaves. Then, as if awakening from a deep sleep or lethargy, he exclaimed:

Land of the blacks, cradle of poor Arsène!
Does your memory come to stir my heart?
Is it the sweet breath of Africa, upon this breeze,
That caresses me and soothes my pain?
Do the trade winds carry my mother's kisses,
Or the songs that console my father?
Dance on, play on, sweet white children;
Your virtue depends on your tender age!

Captured black man, back bent upon the shore,
I see you laughing as you dream of death;
Your liberated soul will float upon a cloud
Back to that fateful native land.
Heaven will restore your mother's embrace
And the music that your father taught you.
Dance on, play on, sweet white children;
Your virtue depends on your tender age!

Never has the peaceful black, content in his poverty,
Crossed the seas to trouble your destiny.
Your men do not sob under our inflexible masters.
What have we done to your fathers' gods
That you steal us from our mothers' arms?
Dance on, play on, sweet white children,
Your virtue depends on your tender age!

"Sarah heard his lament one day. She thought he was singing, just as she liked to do. She came to listen, wrapping her little arms around his neck. When she looked at him, laughing, she saw that he wept. It was the first time she had seen him in tears.

"— You weep! she cried out. Why are you weeping?"

"Not wanting either to deceive Sarah or complain about Silvain, he answered: I was thinking about my mother.

"— What is a mother? Sarah eagerly asked.

"The poor man, troubled by this unforeseen question, remained perplexed.

"— Tell me what a mother is, she insisted.

"After a pause, Arsène replied:

"— A mother is she who cradles us against her breast when we are infants, who suspends us from her body in a sling until we can walk. She sings us to sleep when we cry, finds fruit for us to eat even before we ask, forgetting to eat any herself in order to give it all to us, and suffers when she cannot assuage our hunger.

"He fixed his eyes, filled with sad memories, on the little girl.

"— Then I will call you my mother, she cried, because you have done those things for me.

"Arsène dared say no more. Sarah, whose ideas continued in rapid succession, went on:

"— But if you are weeping for your mother, does that mean that you were once small, my good Arsène?

"— Yes, he said. I was as weak as a newborn lamb. A gentle mother held me to her breast, covered me with kisses, and taught me how to walk. When I knew how to walk, I gamboled around her, and then ventured off

17

all alone to find fruit by myself, so that I could share mine with her. Men like Silvain disembarked on the sand where I was joyfully playing. At first I feared them because they were white, and I tried to flee. But I looked back and found them still there, making signs to offer me objects that I or my mother might desire. When my hands were full of their gifts, they snatched me up in their arms and put me on their ship, where I found other captured black children. We all began crying for our mothers, whom we wanted to see again. But these white men spoke another language and seemed not to understand our entreaties. Indeed they began to laugh as they bound our outstretched hands. I learned later that they planned to sell us. I was sold; I grew up in chains. But often, like today, I remembered the shores of my own land. Perhaps my mother still returns there daily, searching for me and calling out my name. Sometimes I think I hear her voice in the waves that pound ashore, in the murmuring of the great palm trees bending in the wind, in the rapid flight of seabirds overhead.

"Yes, little white girl, everything that is sweet and plaintive, everything that murmurs in my ear, that caresses my brow and cheeks, is the breath and voice of a mother . . . Oh! How I loved her voice!

"Astonishment and sadness clouded Sarah's countenance. When Edwin, who had been seeking his playmate everywhere, found her, her heart was swollen with

Arsène's grief. At first Edwin saw only Sarah's pain, and he demanded to know its cause.

"— He weeps, she replied, pointing to Arsène. Oh, Edwin! If only you knew what a mother is! Do you know?

"— No, said Edwin. "What is it?

"She then apprised him of all she had heard. Edwin listened to her words with the same astonishment she had felt. Imbued with Sarah's glances and the sound of her gentle voice, Arsène's story filled Edwin with deep emotion. Thoughts of play vanished. He shared her sadness. His breast rose; his eyes gazed upon her with a new expression. She stopped speaking. Arsène and the two children looked at each other in silence. Suddenly, all three shivered, hearing Silvain's voice ring out in the air. He soon appeared, calling Arsène back to work.

"Arsène rose to obey and moved away from the children. Mournfully, Sarah followed his movements with her eyes, and then she looked back fearfully at Silvain, who observed the scene with curiosity.

"— Does that slave dare complain? he asked. He is well treated; your father protects him.

"— And he has gained my affection as well, Edwin rejoined. It is thanks to him that we have Sarah. Do not say again that he is a slave, or you will turn me against you.

"— Silvain does not realize that Arsène is unhappy, Sarah said.

"— Am I to blame? the overseer inquired brusquely.

19

"— No, no, she replied. His mother is far away, and he thinks he hears her when the sea rushes toward him, when the wind bends the great palm trees!

"Silvain shrugged with indifference and walked away whistling.

"— Silvain never had a mother, you see; he has no pity for those who miss theirs.

"— Must we have suffered to pity the suffering of others? Oh, I find Silvain hard-hearted. You never had a mother, yet you weep."

"— Yes, she said. The word *mother* fills me with awe. Arsène's story of mothers is beautiful. I want one, Edwin!

"— But I have none to give you, the boy exclaimed. I have no mother! You desire what I lack.

"In despair, he embraced Sarah, who embraced him in turn. Their faces touched like two flowers bowed by the wind beneath a somber sky.

"— Come with me, said Edwin, suddenly inspired by a new idea.

"And overcome with excitement, he ran with her to his father, whose hands he clasped beseechingly.

"— Sarah wants a mother: can you give us one? he implored.

"This unexpected entreaty reached the deepest re-cesses of Mr. Primrose's soul. Drained of all color, he clasped Edwin to his bosom for a few moments.

20

"— My child, I would gladly exchange all my wealth to provide you—to bring back to you—a mother. I have suffered in solitude the misfortune that deprived you of yours. Your mother, whom heaven and your father chose for you, was the kindest and gentlest of mothers, he said finally, in a voice heavy with emotion.

"— What misfortune befell her? cried the frightened child.

"— You will learn the truth one day, Mr. Primrose said, trying to appear calm. One day, Edwin, you will understand the pain that your request has caused me. Today I am unable to respond; never question me again! May your childhood be tranquil: know, my child, that you possess my infinite love and Sarah's friendship. It is too soon for you to make the acquaintance of sorrow. It should remain unknown to children of your age.

"Deeply distressed, he embraced his son and departed. The children dared not follow him. A host of explanations arose in their youthful minds. They concluded with the resolution to obey and remain silent.

"Although time weakened the impression left by this day, although their games resumed when Mr. Primrose's solemn lessons were not occupying their minds, the episode nevertheless marked their tender minds with a melancholy that dampened the turbulence of their youth. Silvain, wishing perhaps to act prudently, softened his behavior toward poor Arsène, who, working primarily

21

in the house from that point on, could be closer to the white children, could speak and listen to them. Arsène considered himself fortunate and breathed more easily."

Adolescence

"Sarah and Edwin grew up like two small trees watered by a life-sustaining spring. During their lessons, Edwin was often distracted, gazing at Sarah rather than listening to his father. But when they were alone, he asked her to recount everything she had learned. Then the important lessons engraved themselves in his heart. It was thus with all the words that Sarah uttered. Their serene innocence made every day as beautiful in their eyes as they were to each other. In the gardens, on the plantation, atop the mountain, everywhere they ran together, Sarah nourished Edwin's imagination. He found her graces reflected everywhere; he compared everything to her.

"One evening he said to her, Look at these two streams that spring from hidden sources. They meet below in the valley of shadows. Their waters join, murmur, and circulate together around our peaceful island. They flow gently, without turbulence, because they find in their path only even sand and flexible plants. Meeting no obstacle, they arrive clear and pure at the coast, where the sea welcomes them into her depths. My father says that this is the destiny of all streams. For you, they provide a mirror that reflects your lovely image. When I look, I see you there with me. Like those streams, we will always be together. Our souls will flow through happy days, and then together we will journey on to a new and more beautiful life, more vast than this unknown sea, whose boundaries we cannot fathom.

"— Yes, Sarah said. Your father told us that this happiness is God's promise. But do you truly heed your father's words? You hardly listen. I often sense, when I see you looking at me, that you want to be out running! You want me to pay less attention to my books. You await impatiently the moment when you can lead me outside with you. I hear you breathing faster as if to move forward the hands of the clock. Only when we are free to sing and run do you ask what your father read to us. Yet the next day, when you repeat his lessons, you have retained more than I have. You astound me, Edwin. How do you learn all that he says?

"— Oh Sarah! I absorb every word you say. Your slightest utterance sparks a throng of ideas, just as a few seeds cast to the wind at random can enrich thousandfold the earth that receives them. Yes, my ideas are born from yours; I await them. Yes, Sarah, I must hear your words and your reminders of my father's lessons. Only then can I learn what he wishes me to know.

"Sarah had reached her thirteenth birthday, without knowing whether she would one day command or obey. But perhaps her charm derived from the profound ignorance

23

that was maintained regarding her destiny. She was in this world to love; that is all that she knew about herself. To be cherished was all she wanted from others. And those who knew her say that they loved her. They say that if her face seemed so beautiful, it was because it was the transparent veil of her soul; that if her skin seemed so white, it was because it blended with the soft muslin of her clothing; that if the blacks called her 'doux zombi la montagne' (the good spirit of the mountain),[2] it was because of the celestial expression that animated her angelic face.

"Mr. Primrose walked down to the shore every day where, at exactly the same hour, an old black man awaited him in a canoe and rowed him silently to Cemetery Island. For fifteen years, this was the most precious moment in days that were otherwise so long. He believed that these were sacred occasions in which his wife reached out to assuage his feelings of regret. Afterward, he went back to meet the old man, who awaited him in his boat to take to the other shore. *Tomorrow* was the only word spoken during these mysterious outings.

---

[2] Desbordes-Valmore here makes one of the first European literary references to the zombie, now familiar from Haitian voodoo as the living dead. An 1809 ethnographic text on Haiti, the *Voyages d'un naturaliste* by Descourtilz, contextualizes a *zomby* (2: 172) or a *zombie* (220) as a ghost or revenant that inspires fear or horror. In Desbordes-Valmore's usage, however, *zombie* appears equivalent to "spirit," connoting positive ethereal qualities, at least as applied to Sarah.

"During his daily absences, Edwin, Sarah, and the faithful Arsène waited for him at the gate of the plantation, breathing in the fresh, light breeze that rustled the large banana leaves under which they sat. One day, Mr. Primrose's book lay near them, and Edwin opened it. His eyes were soon riveted to it, as they often were to Sarah's gaze. Surprised to see him reading so intently, she sought to recapture his attention by singing, while in the distance Arsène played the *bamboula*,[3] an instrument sweet to the ear of the African.

"Edwin suddenly cried out:

"— How beautiful this book is! It teaches so many things! What a bright light it sheds on things! Listen, Sarah: *Heaven wants man to have a companion and to give her the name of spouse: it wants man to be everything for her, as she is everything for him.* The book says so! What a joy it would be to have you for a companion, for a spouse, Sarah!

"— And for a sister, Sarah added timidly.

"— You are not my sister, he answered passionately, I would die if you were.

"— How can it be! A name that was so dear to you in the past now makes you wish to die? she asked in amazement.

---

[3] Descourtilz defines the *bamboula* as "a drum used for dancing" (2: 196). Through the close association of the drum with dancing, *bamboula* also came to be used metonymically as the name for a dance.

"— In the past, Sarah, you were not what I see before my eyes now. Yes! Now you are greater than a sister, and more beautiful! Listen again: *The man's companion is a thousand times more for him than a sister to whom he can never give the name of spouse.* Oh Sarah, I rejoice at not being your brother!

"Astonished by his words, Sarah let the young man hold her hand while he reread aloud the page containing their destiny. Arsène had stopped playing his instrument to listen.

"He listened because even the simplest beings understand love, because its spark rekindles their dormant feelings, because the eyes of two young lovers have a language whose sweetness touches even those who have never loved.

"Silvain felt it too. He saw in the young Creole girl's eyes a love different from the love of gold. To Sarah's misfortune, her tender glance, seeking out and calling to Edwin's eyes only, met the manager's bold eye. He found her look very lovely; the expression it conveyed inflamed his heart and gave him hope. Believing himself to be in love, he rapidly calculated that it was in her best interest to please him. But could Sarah's mysterious birth allow her to aspire to such a union? Was she really just a protected slave? Pondering these questions, he said to himself: 'Her perfect whiteness seems to attest to her free birth; no mixture alters its purity. I see it flush proudly

26

over her cheeks when I punish Arsène. Is she really just an unknown orphan of foreign origins? Mr. Primrose's benevolence toward her suggests that some secret tie unites them. But if he dares not admit their bond and openly recognize her, who deserves her more than I? What better way for him to ensure her happiness than to give her to me with a rich dowry? Such is my just reward for having watched over his property, which he neglects, and which I have a right to share. What better way to prove his generosity toward her than to hand over part of his fortune to a man of great merit who is willing to share his name and rank in society with her? A man who has made himself hated for Mr. Primrose's sake for fifteen years, giving Mr. Primrose all the time in the world to make himself loved?'

"Silvain became obsessed with these thoughts. They came to him in his sleep, they followed him through his days, in his thrice daily review of the vast fields. They made him more active in punishing and counting the slaves, whom he now saw as perhaps his own someday. At first his plan to marry Sarah ripened in silence; then one day he dared to reveal it to his master. He pressed Mr. Primrose adroitly, exaggerated the services he had rendered him, and finally named the price he expected to obtain in return.

"Blinded by his infinite benevolence, Mr. Primrose submitted to Silvain's will, little suspecting him to be a

27

jealous and mercenary man who had usurped his trust through false zeal. Oblivious to the overseer's brazen trickery, the downcast and distracted Mr. Primrose welcomed Silvain's proposal as a source of good fortune for his dear orphan.

"— Well, he said, if she consents, she shall be yours. I will give you her hand. It would seem, Silvain, that you truly deserve her.

"From this instant, Silvain saw himself as Sarah's husband. He went away triumphantly, his head held high, burning to protect her, preparing himself for his new, dignified role. What surprise, what gratitude he counted on reading in the young girl's wide eyes! His impatience gave him wings to climb the mountainside more rapidly. He seemed to say to those he met on the path:

"— You must not detain me. A beautiful girl counts on me to make her happy and myself rich.

"He looked for Sarah, and found her reading at Edwin's side, almost leaning against him. Silvain caught the tender, lively glance she directed at Edwin instead of him, and his ideas were thrown into chaos. His mind filled with jealousy even more rapidly than it had earlier with hope. In a loud voice, he called Arsène, insulted him, and struck him for the first time. Horrified, Sarah begged for mercy, even though she knew not what fault Arsène was accused of committing. The irritated overseer looked at her angrily, responding to her plea only by pushing away the black man, who was stupefied by this strange fury.

"Edwin rose, filled with indignation, and ordered Arsène to remain.

"— Silvain, he said, forbear from pushing Arsène away. Sarah wants him to be near her. Obey Sarah! Second only to my father, she is everything here. She has been my sister and will be my wife. I am her support against evildoers and against you!

"Lightning could not have struck down the manager's audacity more promptly than did these words. He remained petrified by the masterful tone that accompanied them, and anger alone now raged in his eyes. Humiliated for the first time, and by a child, he swallowed this affront, all the more bitter because it was witnessed by the mysterious young girl he already saw as his wife, which was to say his servant.

"One can imagine the atrocious smile that spread across his trembling lips at the idea of revenge. Returning down the mountainside as rapidly as he had climbed it, he ran to catch up with Mr. Primrose's retreating footsteps.

"At first, he could barely speak. His brow, which he wiped to try to give order to the ideas that were assailing him, seemed about to explode. Believing he merely sighed, he roared. He tried to flatter his master, even though he yearned to tear his master's son from limb to

29

limb. Finally, the passion he called love, and which by now was nothing more than hate, poisoned his gestures and revelations. Mr. Primrose listened and contemplated the man who stood before him. The planter's noble face, always sweet and grave, took on the hue of new sorrow. Not enraged as was the evil overseer, he nevertheless suffered the pangs of bitter surprise. Silvain believed he saw in Mr. Primrose's expression the proof of his perverse suspicions about Sarah's birth. He felt he could insist on the fulfillment of the promise he had received that very day. He exaggerated the dangers of delaying, and the tenacity of his demands wrested from Mr. Primrose a decision about the fate of poor Sarah. She would be wretched. She would be Silvain's wife."

Slavery

"Sarah, for her part, was confounded by the storm that had been unleashed. The odious look that Silvain directed at her intimated dire consequences for Arsène, but she kept silent for fear of antagonizing Edwin. In her chagrin, she coldly turned away from him, and that evening he felt a sorrow that he had never experienced before. He wanted to follow her but no longer dared. He felt his heart beat with an unfamiliar violence. Edwin was no longer a child, and it required great restraint for him to withdraw to his room that night after she disappeared down the long gallery of the house.

"No one slept that night on the plantation. Edwin dreamed that he was still reading next to Sarah, and in his sleep he offered her a thousand times the precious names concealed in his book. Sarah listened in silence, and stowed his words away in her soul as a precious gift. These names then troubled but also enchanted her sleep. Silvain, avaricious as ever, felt his heart beat wildly now that he recognized his young master as a rival.

"Mr. Primrose, belatedly repentant, searched for a means of fulfilling his duties as father and benefactor without harshness. He recognized that a good deed often entails great sacrifices, but for the first time he was uneasy about the benevolent act he had performed. When day broke, he was still plunged in a state of uncertainty.

"Wanting to believe that he was needlessly alarmed by his son's feelings for Sarah, flattering himself that Silvain had exaggerated those feelings and that Sarah was too simple to understand or respond to them, he now desired to question her, or rather to announce to her the change he was preparing for her future. Unable to find peace within himself, he thought he would go forth to find Sarah, whom he knew to be accustomed to rising at daybreak. Sarah had indeed gone down to the garden, where she was feeding some of the island's birds. Never before had he truly seen her ravishing face, made only more lovely by the previous day's emotion, her svelte waist, her delicate charms, her eyes, which mirrored the blue of the sky. He paused.

31

A feeling of justice made him think that it was inevitable that Edwin, who had not known Jenny, would love this sweet and decent creature. Sarah, catching sight of him, ran forward, full of blithe trust, holding in her hands fresh flowers that she offered him because they were beautiful. Never had Edwin's father been more dear to her than at this moment when, trying to enlighten her, he was about to destroy her happy and grateful spirit. He gently brushed aside the flowers she offered and seated her beside him.

"— Sarah, he said, listen to me. The interest you inspire in me has not awaited this moment alone to prepare your happiness; but it is time to ensure it. Twelve years have passed since the day when you found in me a refuge, a friend. But my friendship is not enough for the future. Time could deprive you of my care, for you are very young, Sarah, and I am no longer so. Whatever will eventually cause our separation, your grief must be borne in the company of a spouse.

"At this word, Sarah was overcome with emotion, as if Edwin's voice had pronounced the word again. Never guessing that it could designate someone other than Edwin, she lowered her eyes, filled with love, and fell to her knees before Mr. Primrose, with an expression of joy that surprised and charmed him.

"— I see that Silvain was not mistaken, exclaimed Mr. Primrose. It is true, then, that you will be happy with him and will cherish the bonds that unite you to him?

32

"Sarah, still kneeling, gazed at Mr. Primrose with eyes that now expressed only doubt and fear. But her fear, modest like her joy, found neither voice nor breath. She waited for him to speak again, hoping to have misunderstood him.

"— Silvain merits his good fortune, he continued, for he has promised me yours. It gives me consolation to think, dear Sarah, that heaven, which brought you to this island, wanted you to find refuge here: first in me and in my house, and now in a spouse, a man whom I respect enough that I am willing to grant his wish to marry you. Obey me, and you will find happiness.

"He arose, eager to take his leave so that Sarah would not have to put in words feelings that he assumed to be favorable to his wishes. But she cried out in a passionate and heartfelt voice:

"— I am not Silvain's sister, sir! Heaven did not give me to him but to you, Edwin's father. I will be Edwin's wife, because you granted me to him when I was an infant. What! How could Silvain be my husband? I do not want him.

"Mr. Primrose was shocked by Sarah's forthright response, although it had escaped her lips with such truthful immediacy that he did not have the heart to take offense. Nevertheless, he resolved to reassert firmly the submission owed to him by her and his son, who was not destined for such a marriage. He ended by affirming his paternal authority over both of them, telling her that if they did not leave their destinies in his hands they would offend God by offending him.

"— This cannot be true, Sarah responded naively. God blessed me, through you. How can he now wish to cause me such harm? Oh! no—she continued, clasping her hands—you must not give Sarah as a wife to anyone else but Edwin. Surely you will choose me to make him happy, as he has been in our childhood, which has barely come to an end. You will not sacrifice my youth to Silvain, who frightens me. I would prefer to take my own life.

"Mr. Primrose trembled at words that resounded as poignantly in his mind as Jenny's name.

"— Sarah, he said sadly, take more care with your words. The one who has protected you from your earliest childhood cannot wish for your death. In enlightening your spirit, in teaching you virtue, in shielding you from the dangers and the servitude to which you would have been consigned by your parents' abandonment, I have replaced them. Can you ask for more? Is hurting me a just recompense for all the care I have given you? I have had the pleasure of protecting you from a thousand misfortunes. Does that give you the right to ask me to sacrifice my wishes, my plans for the future, my hopes, all of which reside in my son? Is it not just to expect that he be separated in the future from you, Sarah, a stranger to us?

"— Is that what you think? cried Sarah, mournfully. Am I a stranger when I breathe only to love you? Can I create a new soul for myself? Can the future turn my memories away from you and Edwin? Could I ever give others the respect and love with which I repay your benevolence?

"— But, Mr. Primrose replied, others may merit your love and respect. Would you be so unjust as to disdain them? You seem to take pleasure in dwelling in sadness. I repeat that I only want to change your situation by making you independent of myself, who will not live forever.

"Sobs were Sarah's only response to Mr. Primrose's continued arguments that she should be happy marrying Silvain. He took her silence as a first sign of submission, and he left her feeling, if not more satisfied, at least no longer concerned that her pure and upright spirit would oppose him.

"How could she have responded? A gloomy light had now revealed the lonely path on which she had formerly walked with such assurance. Looking to the past, she saw images that used to be vague but that now filled her with fear. Where was she brought from on the day of her earliest memories, when Edwin as a child appeared before her? Where did she come from? Who brought her into the world? Why had she been born if not for Edwin? At the same time, her whole being shuddered at the thought of defying Mr. Primrose, of seeing sorrow in eyes and hearing reproach in a voice that had always been so indulgent toward her. Oh! Her benefactor's anger threatened to provoke God's wrath. She bent her head in submission.

"— I must obey, she said to herself. I must go down on my knees and beg forgiveness for ever having dared think that life is happiness. I must concede his right to condemn me to a life of suffering in silence under the most dreadful of authorities, that of Silvain. Alas! If I become his wife, if he orders me to love him the way I love Edwin, what will I say? His voice is so harsh, so frightening! It will only wound my heart and disturb the cherished image of Edwin that resides there, hidden under layers of tears and regrets.

"Sarah had stayed motionless for some time when Silvain, having spied upon his master and seen him descending to the shore with his son, suddenly appeared before her. She could not keep herself from shuddering, which offended the proud overseer. He was already insulted by everything he had heard, and the smile that he forced himself to paste across his visage only gave him a wild look. The terms 'stranger' and 'servitude' that Mr. Primrose had pronounced transformed her in his eyes into a poor foundling, only rescued from extreme misfortune by the compassion she had inspired in her master. Thus instead of refraining from humiliating her, he gave free rein to the expression of his rage.

"— So you want no part of me, he said, preventing her from fleeing. You refuse my hand! Must one own two hundred slaves to gain favor in your eyes, proud pauper? Well, I foresaw this. It is the price of ill-advised benevolence. It is what can be expected from treating slaves with too much indulgence.

"— Slaves! said Sarah, filled with horror.

"— What else might you be? replied Silvain. Where, pray tell, are your parents? Where is your homeland? Where are your possessions? The only person who knows you is an old slave. No one else claims you or is worried about your existence, except for this miserable black man who came to beg for the refuge and pity that you are abusing today by loving the son of your master and inciting his hatred against those who deserve to be respected.

"— My God! said Sarah, leaning against a tree. I am a slave! And I knew nothing of my condition. I knew nothing!

"— Yes, thanks to your master's weakness, said Silvain. He has sought to spare you the truth, because of its harshness. I reveal it to open your eyes, to bring you back to your duties, which you have forgotten.

"— Oh Silvain! cried Sarah. How your terrible revelation causes me pain!

"Silvain countered. — It was my duty to make you understand the fate I have chosen for you. You should bless it, not show disdain.

"— Less than ever! Sarah retorted. I shall bless your cruelty less than ever. I have learned from you that I am a slave! But that does not make me yours, tyrant. The man who was charitable enough never to have mortally wounded me with this awful name will be charitable enough not to give me to a master like you.

"— So you fear me more than death, Silvain replied with biting mockery.

"— That's right, Sarah cried out in despair. I embrace death; it delivers slaves.

"Far from being touched by the pitiful accent with which she pronounced these words, the unworthy man congratulated himself on having broken her will, and he went away content.

"I have punished her, he thought. I have killed a dangerous presumptuousness in her. Mr. Primrose will be grateful.

"He sought thus to countervail what he called his master's weakness. He was certain that his strategy would enable him to obtain Sarah. His avarice trumped the humiliation of being hated. Gold alone would compensate for the loss of his hopes, and Sarah's value to him depended on her becoming his wife. He also knew that Mr. Primrose had chosen Edwin's wife, who had been raised in England, and that father and son would soon return there. The manager would then be solely responsible for the properties he coveted with such passion. To be no more than the guardian of those properties seemed unbearable to him. More than once he had thrilled at the thought that he held his master's entire fortune in his hands. Mere humility had kept him satisfied with only a part when others in his place would have taken the whole. Such ideas, which obsessed him, seemed to await this propitious moment to stifle the remnants of his honor and lead him into crime.

"Sarah, alone and horrified, repeated over and over:

"— A slave! I am a slave! I must have learned of my condition too late, because this abjection only makes me more aware of my pride. Arsène, Arsène! When you bemoaned your loss of freedom, were you also weeping for mine? Dear Arsène, you should have told me the truth. I would have learned to weep as you do and perhaps resign myself to this slavery whose very name fills me with horror today!"

Isle of Shades

"Edwin had spent the whole day far from Sarah. Hoping to wean him away from the habit of never leaving Sarah's side, his father had sent him to the town. Edwin now returned, breathless with impatience and consumed with the desire to recount to her the story of his sorrow. He longed to tell her all the thoughts and events of an entire day spent without her. His surprise was great at not finding her running to meet him, and then, when he encountered her at last, at seeing her only tremble in response to the demonstrations of joy that were even more evident in his features than his words. At first, having brushed aside her curls and seeing her so pale, he thought that his absence had undermined her health. He swore to her a thousand times that he would never leave her again.

"— Since a woman's duty is to follow her husband everywhere, he said, you will always accompany me when I go to the village and wherever else my father might send me. Be happy again, dear Sarah! One sad day, a thousand times longer than any other, is enough.

"When Edwin took her hands away from her face and found that it was bathed in tears, his heart stopped beating for a moment. Overwhelming her with a hundred questions at once, in which anger already mingled with tenderness, he pressed her, begged her, ordered her to reveal to him the cause of her tears.

"The mixture of authority, submission, sweetness, and vehemence in Edwin's voice troubled Sarah to such a point that, weeping, she stammered in a jumble of words the terrible news she had received. Edwin, believing that he must be mad as he listened to her, did not even endeavor to stop her when she slipped out of his arms and cried out in a broken voice:

"— Yes! I am a slave!

"He remained thunderstruck for several moments, but his fury against Silvain soon restored him to his senses. He tore around the plantation, calling for his father and demanding to see him with loud cries. Finally discerning the path Silvain had taken, he hastened with the speed of an unleashed torrent to catch up with him, shouting:

"— Miserable wretch, ingrate! You will pay dearly for her tears!

"Silvain, who saw him and guessed his intent, ran off in all haste to take out his anger on some innocent slave.

"Edwin then ran along the shore in such confusion that with each passing figure he thought he had found his father and cried out from afar:

"— Wait! Father!

"No one answered, and he resumed his frantic course. Finally, a black boy who was fishing on the bank said that he had seen Mr. Primrose cross over to the other shore in the old oarsman's canoe. Edwin jumped into the boat of the boy, who, stunned, watched him row away.

"Obsessed with the urgency of his trouble, forgetting that he had orders never to follow his father on his mysterious outings, Edwin rapidly gained the other side. Finding the sea unable to match the pace of his impatience, he leaped from the bark even before it hit the sand.

"Landing on the little island for the first time, he searched for some dwelling, but saw only tombs and melancholy trees. The old black man, lying in his canoe, was unable to tell him where his master was; and poor Edwin, seeing no one else to ask, set off on a path where he thought he saw the fresh imprint of a man's footsteps. But he was soon lost, for the wind dispersed the sand on which the footprints were traced. Overcome with grief, parched from the heat, he stopped for a few moments to recover his breath. The vague sound of a voice floated to him upon the breeze; the rising moon guided him among the paths and the sharp-leaved plants that covered them. He arrived at last at a place where the ground was even and covered with thornbushes, where the scent of acacias and orange trees freshened the air and brought a breath of life to this asylum of death.

"Mr. Primrose was on his knees, praying. His son, so filled with pain and the need to convey it, forgot his grief, gazing at his father with religious fear. He gently parted the branches of the trees that sheltered this place like a dark curtain. He contemplated lengthily and in silence this friend of his youth, the arbiter of his destiny, prostrate before a tomb, his brow touching the earth. Overcome by grief, he too fell to his knees and prayed for his father. The sound of rustling leaves from his movements attracted Mr. Primrose's attention; he saw Edwin at the other side of the tomb.

"Moonlight washed across Edwin's face. The transformation of his features, now as gentle and pale as Jenny's, profoundly moved Edwin's father. He stood up and extended his hand in silence, troubled by his son's unexpected presence. Edwin pressed his father's hand to his lips and covered it with tears without daring to break the silence between them. Mr. Primrose embraced him and, for the first time, allowed himself to weep in his son's arms.

"— Dear Edwin! he exclaimed. I have dreaded this moment that makes you a partner in my grief. I have carried its sorrowful weight alone for fifteen years. I need a friend with whom to share it. Become that friend, my son, and carry half the burden of my pain. But with this sad gift comes the further burden of sparing me other sorrows. I add no reproach to the trust I now place in you. But I remind you of my admonition, which you forgot, not to follow me here; and I remind you that a father's orders always have as their sole ambition the repose and happiness of his children. Do you remember the day you asked me for a mother? I was unable then to show you your mother's final resting place, as I do today. This refuge is not suited to children. Strong emotions can be harmful in childhood, when an ardent sensibility internalizes them too profoundly. Knowing your disposition, I awaited the full awakening of your reason to help you sustain the blow I must subject you to by bringing you to the tomb of the mother who lost her life giving you yours. Judge for yourself how I value your life after what it cost me! Whatever your reasons for thwarting my tender precautions, you must tearfully explain them now to your mother. My tears have spoken to her of you for fifteen years. Every evening here, your mother, a model of virtue and love, has from beyond the tomb heard me speak your name.

"Edwin's trembling knees no longer obeyed him. He fell almost lifeless at the feet of his father, who lifted him up and pressed him to his heart, where Edwin stayed a long time as if in a faint. He tried in vain to echo Mr. Primrose's last words. He wanted to name his mother but knew not how. When he summoned the strength to speak, he said, sighing deeply:

"— Oh my father, did she look like Sarah?

"— She cannot be compared to anyone, my son!

"Edwin dared not pursue his questioning, and Mr. Primrose was also quiet for a few moments. Then he added:

"— Our families were united; our fortunes were equal; our union fulfilled the dearest wishes of her parents and mine. This is how marriage is approved by the world and by God, my son. Yours has been decided for a very long time. In England, to which we will soon travel together, you will find the precious girl from your mother's family who is destined for you. That family still grieves for Jenny and yearns to see her again in you. My weakness alone has for so long kept me from selling my property and returning to England, where these dear relations await us. The thought of wresting myself from this dear tomb, of abandoning the soil that has been my whole world for sixteen years, throws my spirit into inexpressible agony. I have never been able to summon the courage to perform this final sacrifice. But it must be done! It must!—he continued, drawing his son toward the shore. —Your visit here today heralds my farewell to her.

"Edwin's astonishment, the incomprehensible future that stretched out before him, the succession of deep emotions that he had just experienced, left him weak and speechless. The motive for his frantic search was now locked away in his soul. He let himself be led back by Mr. Primrose, walking at his side, silent and with lowered head, in the most complete despondency.

"But just as they were about to return to the plantation, the sound of Silvain's strident voice stopped him in his tracks: it reminded him of Sarah's tears. Seizing his father's hands, he forced him to stop also.

"— Is it true, O my father, he implored, that Silvain dares to love her? That he is authorized by you to speak as her master? Is it true, he added despairingly, that she is a slave?

"Mr. Primrose, alarmed by Edwin's unexpected emotion, which seemed almost delirious, responded gently but firmly that Sarah was only a slave to her duty, as we all are. Duty, he explained, is a severe but fair taskmaster, and thus one should always be happy to obey it.

"— Alas! It is you, my father, who makes it her duty to leave us! Must misery be her duty and mine as well? And to aggravate her misery, you choose to place her under the authority of a horrid man who inspires her with fear and me with hatred.

"— But why do you hate him, my son? Why does she fear him? Silvain has a brusque manner, but he has integrity. He serves me with boundless zeal. His probity merits our trust.

"— He will cause her death, the barbarian! He has treated her like a slave!

"— Do you believe that, Edwin?

"— Do I believe it? Sarah herself told me so.

"He then embraced his father's knees so ardently, addressed him so respectfully, expressed his touching plea so tearfully that Mr. Primrose, who was displeased with Silvain for what he had just heard, could resist no longer: he promised to give Sarah the right to refuse the overseer, if she persisted in her antipathy for him.

"— Do you swear it, Father? asked Edwin gravely.

"— I promise it, my son; and you, for your part, must promise to obey. Promises are vows made by friends. I want no other kind between us.

"Edwin, although he shuddered at this promise, felt only gratitude for what he had obtained. At least Sarah, the sole object of his concern, was not a slave. Odious Silvain would no longer make her tears flow. He dried his tears then, and although his heart remained burdened with affliction for his own fate, the most painful burden had fallen away."

Narcisse

"Sarah, yielding to an anxiety that no hope could calm, stayed in her room. She trembled at the thought of reappearing before Mr. Primrose, who was now fixed in her imagination in the same light in which she had seen him the night before. Even Edwin was no longer her Edwin: he was a master. As soon as she heard the two of them returning, she ran to hide behind the curtains, as frightened and confused as if they had actually appeared before her. After straining her ears for a considerable time, and hearing, in the deep calm, only the thudding of her heart, which beat with suffocating force, she left her hiding place. She found that her brow was burning with shame; the word 'slave' seemed to be inscribed upon it. Only before God could she keep from blushing. Before God one feels shame only for crimes actually committed. Thus the wretched feel less abject in solitude; they weep, but without shame.

"Yet the night was stifling and afforded no rest. Awaiting sleep, Sarah could not close her eyes, and agitation eventually gave her the courage to leave her room. She arose without a sound and put on her light dress. Then, opening the wooden shutters, she slipped easily through the window that overlooked the mountains and began to walk, asking heaven to guide her to Arsène's cabin. There, she opened the door and called out softly.

"Arsène, whose sleep was heavy with exhaustion, awoke with difficulty. Seeing in the starlight this young girl dressed in white, he fell to his knees, crossing his arms before his face with great anguish. He had taken her, as he himself later admitted, for the ghost of a young woman whose death he had witnessed.

"— It is me, my good Arsène, said Sarah tremulously. I wanted to speak to you without anyone's hearing us. Fear not; it is only Sarah.

"As soon as Arsène heard this voice, he stood up, no longer afraid. He waited for her to speak; but Sarah only looked at him indecisively, instead of addressing him. She sat down on the reed mat that served the black man as a bed, and he knelt again before her.

"— I thought you would be sleeping at this hour, he told her.

"—No, she answered, sleep has forsaken me tonight. But you, good Arsène, were you dreaming of your mother again?

"— Always, for she may still be unhappy!

"— Tell me about my own mother, please.

"— Your mother, little white girl, he answered in a desolate tone, your mother is well, for she is in heaven, the home of those who have suffered.

"— Then I will see my mother again! the orphan said to herself, and began to cry. The black man remained silent, and Sarah went on:

"— There is so much you have hidden from me! No doubt you were afraid to burden me when I was still so small and happy, too fragile for such sad secrets. But give me my secrets: give them to me, Arsène! I already know that happiness passes like childhood, I already know that I am a slave.

"— Heavenly father! cried the astonished black man. Where did you get that terrible idea? Did I not sell my freedom to save yours?

"— Is that true? exclaimed Sarah, seizing Arsène's hands with alacrity. You sold yourself for me? I am free! Silvain lied to me! Tell me quickly, tell me everything I owe you! I may die from the joy and pain I am feeling. But I shall bless you if I can die free! And yet . . . Refrain from telling me! If you spared me the awful name 'slave' at the price of your own freedom, my savior, how could I survive the grief of seeing you bear that name for me?

"— Softly, softly, Arsène admonished her, mingling his own sobs with hers. At this hour Silvain may be awake. We must shed our tears in silence.

"— Where did you take me from, when you brought me to Edwin? she asked, keeping her voice low. Do not hesitate any longer! Tell me about my mother![4]

"— I took you from her arms only when they stopped clasping you against a heart that had ceased to suffer. You already know how I fell into the hands of the whites. A rich master bought me from my abductors. And may God forgive me for speaking the truth: he was as bad as they were. But he had a young son endowed with natural goodness. The son saved me from punishments that I, in my impatience with slavery, brought upon myself. I uttered piercing cries when they called me 'slave,' even though I hardly complained about the blows that sometimes rendered my body powerless. I watched my blood flow with a dry eye, and I said: 'Me free!' This courage so irritated the fury of my old master that he kept redoubling the terrible punishment he had inflicted on me. His son was so moved that through his entreaties, and above all through his promises to make me understand my fate, they gave me up to his care. The gentleness of this young man's manners triumphed by degrees over my hatred for the whites. One day they had left me for dead under a tree, where I was waiting silently for my soul, already

---

[4] The singular lack of paragraph breaks in Arsène's response to Sarah's question may have symbolic valences, drawing attention to the storytelling culture that evolved among slaves in the New World, or to the flow of words and feelings inspired by the subject of the maternal.

poised to take flight on my lips, to depart for *Guinée*;[5] for this hope pursues us in captivity and often counsels us to flee our condition. I was surprised when he addressed consoling words to me. I was indeed so surprised by his charitable voice that my chest heaved and I looked at him submissively. I examined his features and his eyes with curiosity; and as there was nothing threatening about them, I believed that he was another species of man, one I did not yet know. He soon obtained my most absolute obedience. He so won over my heart, embittered by the sadness of no longer seeing my mother, that I attended upon him with love, without thinking that I was serving him. I was probably a few years younger than he; I do not know my exact age. He took pleasure in enlightening me on matters about which I was ignorant. He was pleased above all to see me happy, because all the slaves on the plantation had a morose air that afflicted him. I danced to please him, but only when we were alone, for his father's severity made a crime of the most innocent pastimes. I soon realized that the son was becoming dreamy and restless. Often, mysteriously, he made me wait for him in the same place; and I was alone for long periods, guarding the books, the nets, or the weapons that were the pretext for our outings. But as we always came back

---

[5] *Guinée* was the African diasporan term for both "Africa" and "afterlife" or "paradise."

empty-handed, as our stocks of powder and lead never diminished, his father became suspicious and had him followed by a less faithful servant than I. His report was the ruin of my master. It was now known that he had fallen in love with a young Creole girl. She was free. But her father was so poor that he was obliged to cultivate a little patch of ground that barely sufficed to nourish them. His daughter tended the cabin and prepared the rice that he gathered for the two of them. At first my master had been unable to see her without pity. But as he began to love her, he realized that his sentiment did not derive from pity. She loved him in turn. God seemed to bless their love, although later, he abandoned them, as you will see. O Sarah! The father of my young master fell into a fury upon learning the news of their love. He was so enraged that it seemed he would die. Everyone trembled for the young girl and for his son, who never denied the great love he felt for her. As soon as my master had admitted that he wanted her and no other to be his wife, his father began to treat him as pitilessly as the slaves. But the father's inhuman actions only increased his son's love for the beautiful Narcisse, just as they increased our desire for freedom. No longer able to see her, he fell into a mortal languor. Trying to console him, as he had consoled me, I repeated the sweet, tender words I had learned from him. He was touched by my efforts, and I could see that he loved me the more for it, since he sent me in secret to Narcisse, who came to trust me. I ran furtively to tell her that her absence made my master weep, and I carried back to him the news that she was weeping far from him. I came back one evening with news that was sadder still: the father of this young girl had died the night before. I had found her so grief-stricken that my legs failed me as I ran to inform my master. This new misfortune touched him more than all the rest. Looking at me, perhaps forgetting for the moment who I was, he begged for my permission to leave, as if he took me for his father! Although those who feared being punished by his father watched his every movement, they loved him too much to want to harm him; and thus he was able to see his dear Narcisse once more. Together they wept. But this sad happiness was troubled again, and then destroyed forever. My unfortunate master was surprised by his father in person, who wanted to kill him at the feet of this tender girl. She only obtained the father's mercy by falling to her knees, swearing to renounce the son in this world. Alas! She kept her word! But his cruel father, who believed neither in promises nor in love, separated them with violence. A few days later, my master's father was so barbarous as to have his son placed aboard a ship headed for Europe: a ship so well guarded that he seemed no less a slave than are we. All that he was able to obtain on leaving his beloved forever was my liberty, by a contract that I read in tears, because it separated me from him.

The night before his departure, I slipped into his room, where, kneeling at his feet, I begged him to bring me with him to serve him and to speak to him of Narcisse every day. He looked at me in consternation and said:

"— Arsène! If you follow me, who will stay with her? Oh! Do not abandon her, my faithful Arsène! You will love me by loving her, you will console me by consoling my better half. Tell her everything that you see in my tears. Do they not show you, Arsène, that I am dying of sadness and that I am dying for her? Tell her to wait for me. I cannot tell her again that I love her and that I will always love her. You must go back and tell her that I swore it to you, before God who hears and judges me.

"Then (my blood stops cold when I remember the scene), he knelt before poor Arsène. My courage must have been great indeed since I did not expire at that very moment.

"I followed him the next day to the port. They hardly needed to use force against him at that point; he was near death. Despite myself I cried out as I watched the launch move away from the bank. I climbed a rock at the edge of the sea, and I was going to hurl myself in to swim after my dear master, when I found Narcisse, stretched out on the rock, pale and motionless. Then I remembered her beloved's final plea. Seeing her thus immobile, I stayed with her until nightfall, overcome with gloom and sorrow.

"When the port was calm and silent, I carried her in my arms to the deserted shore. There, after laying her on the sand, I bathed her brow with water and moistened her dry and discolored mouth. She opened her eyes and turned them toward the vessel that was now far out of sight. She seemed changed to stone on the bank that the tide was overtaking by degrees. A wave engulfed us and threatened to take her with me. Narcisse looked at me with astonishment, and, no doubt out of pity for me, slowly made her way back to the poor cabin. I followed her wordlessly. I slept at her door, where she found me again in the morning. She wanted to speak, but her heart was broken. I saw her despairing gaze directed at the sky. I told her, without changing a word, what my master had told me; I had repeated it to myself all night to avoid forgetting it. She cried bitterly and then seemed calmer.

"During the day, I cultivated the plot of land that had been long neglected. I planted rice there once again. I sought fruits for our nourishment in the woods. In the evening, I followed her to the rock where the moon found her seated silently, while I stood mute before her. One night, she suddenly came out of the cabin to my side: 'Arsène!' she said, hiding her face in her hands, 'Arsène! I am no longer the only one in danger on this island. Save Narcisse and your master's child. Soon it will be impossible for me to hide my condition. His father's fury might wrench from me the living image of the beloved man for whom I will soon die. Save me! Save us!' Sharing her anguish, I fled with her through the hills into the arid part of the island, through shrubs and brush. I returned alone the following night to retrieve the canoe that had belonged to her father. I carried it on my shoulders so that people would believe we had fled the island, although probably no one was concerned with Narcisse, since no one suspected this misfortune. I also carried along everything that could be of use to us in our retreat, where we lived as in a tomb, so deeply hidden that it seemed to exist beyond this life. I only ventured out with caution during the night, to cast my nets in the sea that bordered our solitary camp. Around us I found fruits that replaced the fresh water we sometimes lacked.

"One night, coming back loaded down with provisions, I heard a new voice in the thatched cabin that I had built for Narcisse. This sweet, weak voice was yours, little Sarah, and I saw in your mother's eyes the only ray of joy that had passed through them since my master's departure. She seemed to be restored to life in caring for you, and to forget herself in long periods of contemplating her daughter. But at the same time, death was watching beautiful Narcisse, even though she tried to elude it through her love for you. Death refused to relinquish its hold and came a step closer each day. My young mistress saw it before her in the shadow of the trees and the black rocks that surrounded us. At times her languid hand signaled for me to see death's hand upon her. But I could see only the shadows, the rocks, and the trees. Then her sad look turned to you, where it remained. You were playing next to her when she bade you farewell!

"—The sun is setting for me, she said one evening, carry me out to feel its last rays!— I obeyed her command. She struggled to lift her head. Her body, exhausted the previous evening, seemed to find the strength to escape my arms that enveloped her. The smile that brightened her half-opened lips wrenched my heart. I knew that it was her last. Her soul, now as tranquil as the waning day, joined its dying light. Her eyes widened and shone with a bright glow. Suddenly the glow was extinguished. I hid my head in the dust . . .

"A cry escaped from Sarah's lips. Poor Arsène stopped speaking, silenced by his heartrending memories. Together they wept. But remembering suddenly that dawn was breaking and Silvain might surprise them, the black man stepped out of his cabin to reassure himself that no one had yet arisen on the plantation. He led Sarah back, promising that as soon as they could speak again, he would tell her more about her past and about a project that he had been contemplating for a long time. Sarah, weary and overwhelmed, fell asleep at the hour when she normally awoke. In sleep she saw again the images that Arsène had evoked in her mind."

Arsène's Plan

"Everything had changed in this once peaceful home. Beneath its apparent calm and silence lay trouble, suspicion, and fear. Edwin, despite his father's constant presence, directed painful and penetrating looks at Sarah that she could not bear to see. When they spoke, their voices were so tender that they seemed to reveal their very souls to each other. Their words, meaningless to others, became the exchange of their saddest confessions. Mr. Primrose witnessed their sorrow yet tried, despite his apprehensions, to hasten their separation. While wishing to remain faithful to the promise he had made to his son, he lacked a plan to ensure Sarah's well-being. To bring Sarah with them seemed impossible, but to leave her on the island without support or a fixed situation was, in his eyes, a barbarous act that went against his reason. Thus, all three ceased to speak, their days equally consumed with uncertainty.

"The overseer, whose impatience could not long withstand such reservations, watched his master with somber concern. One day, filled with anger that he could barely control, he came to claim the interview that would determine his fate. In granting Silvain's request, Mr. Primrose little suspected that his own future was also at stake. As he set off for the meeting, he gave Sarah a look in which her duty was written; she rose to obey his mute command. Alone with Edwin for an instant, she was unable to share his joy. She was about to retreat, her eyes lowered, her step unsteady, when he abruptly stepped forward to stop her and said:

"— Here you are, Sarah! Let me look at you! I have not seen you for a long time!

"Sarah, turning her head, neither wanted nor was able to respond.

"— What are you afraid of, he continued, with a searching look, there is no one here.

"— God sees us, she said. I must take leave of you.

"— No, no, I have so much to tell you! Silvain deceived you. You, you are not . . . No, you are not a slave. Whose slave could you be? You are free, do you understand? Free! Free to turn down all the husbands who might offer themselves to you. Will you despise them, Sarah? Will you refuse them?

"She raised her eyes to his, with a look that transmitted her answer directly to his heart. Then Edwin, remembering all his sorrow, revealed to her their misfortune and impending separation.

"— I know everything, she replied, rebuffing him with a weak voice. Let me go.

"— If you know everything, if you know how unhappy I am and how much I love you, how can you leave me? How can you allow me to die of love for you?

"— I refuse to hear your words, cried Sarah, I refuse to heed them or learn from them. I refuse to disobey your father. Now let me leave!

"Loving Edwin as deeply as she did, Sarah had to summon the greatest effort to retreat at that moment. To abandon your beloved as he weeps, without daring to weep with him, is perhaps more difficult than death itself. But her duty, and her mother's example, gave her the strength to break Edwin's heart. Mr. Primrose heard her pass in the gallery and opened the door. When he saw that his son was preparing to follow her, he ordered him sharply to stay where he had left him.

"Edwin turned back, stricken, convinced that God, like Sarah, had abandoned him. Not daring to accuse his father of cruelty, he made her the object of his recriminations. He even saw it as a crime that she was more obedient than he.

"Sarah, dissolving in tears, met Arsène, and beckoned him to follow her. He stepped into her room.

"—More tears, said the faithful black man with a penetrating look. Oh! Cruel white man! These tears speak ill of him. It is time—he continued, staring at the ground—to renew our request for God's mercy.

"Sarah, seeing him deep in reflection, asked what was occupying his thoughts. —So many things weigh on my heart, he said, pointing to it. He stopped, for fear of being overheard, but seeing the door closed, he went on to disclose the information that Sarah wanted to know.

"—Alone with you in our solitary world, I was so despondent that I nearly followed your mother to the grave. But you were there, my little mistress. You could not yet speak, but you cried and searched with your eyes for a mother whom you would never see again. The idea that I too might leave you filled me with such fear that I took you away in my arms, away from that sad little cabin. While scouring the woods, whence I dared venture forth fearfully only when you were not with me, I heard someone call my name. It was the first time in two years that a man's voice had struck my ear. I stopped, seized by surprise. An old maroon slave[6] emerged from the brush where I stood. I recognized him as a slave of my former master's neighbor. Since he was trembling almost as much as I, believing that he was being pursued, my fears abated and I reassured him I would cause him no harm. 'It is not you that I fear,' he said, "but when I heard you in the brush, I thought you were a white.'

"He told me the story of his escape and what had led up to it. By contrast, he was so happy in the woods that he had resolved to die there rather than return to the control of white men. I said the same thing. He informed me that

---

[6] When slaves escaped their masters and fled to the hills or the brush, they became "maroons," living in "maroonage" (in French, le marronage).

nothing had changed since my departure. —Everyone thought, he said, that Narcisse had thrown herself from the rocks where she sat every evening. Some said they saw her fall, and others responded with 'What a shame!' As for you, Arsène, the slaves envied you. We said: 'He should have come celebrate with us before leaving the island.' But others added, 'How could he celebrate, knowing that we remained enslaved.' And nothing more has transpired since then, the unfortunate black man said.

"I was happy to have met him. Once we had said our good-byes, I ran to rejoin you where I had left you sleeping. I feared that your cries would reach the ear of the maroon slave, who might later tire of living in isolation and return to the plantation, as I had seen happen with other runaway blacks. I came to a decision at that very moment. I returned to the abandoned cabin and took anything that could be of use to you. I packed my canoe with all the provisions it could hold: dried fish, roots, and fruit. I then placed our fate in the hands of Providence. After a few days of travel, the exact direction and duration of which remain unknown to me, we came ashore at the foot of this mountain, where God has protected and hidden us for twelve years. I showed Mr. Primrose the document written by my master attesting to my freedom; and I entrusted our fate—yours, my poor white orphan, as well as mine, your only support—to him alone in the world. He promised to take care of you. Since then I may not have fully repaid his hospitality through working and relinquishing my freedom, but I had nothing else to offer.

"See now if you are a slave! Do you think I would ever allow the harsh treatment I have endured from Silvain to be inflicted upon Narcisse's daughter? Believe me, were it not for the fear that you could fall into the hands of him who caused the death of your young and beautiful mother, I would tell all. It is she who made me swear never to return you to anyone other than her unfortunate beloved, should he ever return to look for her. He will come back, Sarah, you will know your father and you will be happy. I have seen it in my dreams. But—he added mysteriously—if something should happen, pray for me and never forget that you are free.

"Hearing Silvain pass by the door muttering angrily, Sarah was unable to respond. As soon as the overseer was far enough away, Arsène hastened down the corridor and ran to join the slaves returning from the fields.

A Betrayal

"Silvain was furious after the audience with his master. Overtly minimizing the defeat he had suffered, in his heart he nurtured it as an incurable wound. Without having either approved or argued against a word of Mr. Primrose's reasoned consideration of the problem, he privately resolved to avenge himself by ruining this honest man. The means to do this appeared so magically that he felt justified by fate.

"Mr. Primrose, who had at last set the date of their departure for England, decided to sell his island properties. Silvain, who relished his status as their only steward, was initially devastated; this decision seemed to destroy all his hopes at once. Upon further reflection, his anger quickly turned to joy. Rather than leave his fortune to chance, he resolved now to take hold of his own destiny. He decided to flee as soon as he had taken possession of the profits from this very substantial sale. Thus motivated, he invested such energetic ardor in the transactions that within a few days his master's worldly goods and the plantation, located in the most beautiful part of the island, had found a new owner.

"Fate had perversely favored the unfaithful servant by bringing a rich Swede and his family from Sainte-Marie[7] to settle in our colony. Silvain saw this man as his best prospect. He found the Swede so impatient to acquire the properties and willing to follow his lead that before long nothing remained to be done but to exchange land, slaves, and contracts for gold.

"The rapid and important negotiations were carried out under Mr. Primrose's eyes. But the man who would succeed him on the plantation was forced to return im-

---

[7] Sainte-Marie is a town in Martinique.

mediately afterward to Saint-Marie to settle his family's fortune and their impending departure. Silvain alerted the buyer to Mr. Primrose's plans to return to England and offered, in order to avoid any delay that could negatively affect the negotiations, to go to Sainte-Marie himself with the purchasing contract and his master's power of attorney. Mr. Primrose gave him everything. The wretch then left, never to return.

"Mr. Primrose, whose thoughts now revolved entirely around his son, thought he should seize the occasion to separate him from Sarah. Silvain was his only confidant. And although Silvain was initially irritated by the plan of being accompanied by Edwin, whom he saw as an obstacle to his own dark intentions, he pretended to welcome it to ensure his imprudent master's trust in him. He took so many precautions that he could have accomplished his trickery beneath Mr. Primrose's very eyes.

"Who could imagine the feelings that gripped Edwin when his father came to awake him when it was time to depart? The presence of Silvain and the Swede, who had come to bid farewell, tied his tongue. He looked at everyone with confusion.

"—You will leave us for only a few days, my son, said Mr. Primrose, putting his arm around his shoulders.

"—Father, you are sending me away, said Edwin softly, and then when I return, we must embark. Twice I must endure the pain of this wrenching departure!

"— Patience, Edwin, answered Mr. Primrose. I must trust your courage lest I begin to doubt my own.

"Edwin fell silent, defeated by the kindness of his father's entreaty. His pale expression alone dared communicate a reproach to his virtuous father.

"But alas! What could he say to Sarah, whom he perceived standing before the window that he passed on his way to the port? He stopped amid the men escorting him, grabbed Silvain's arm, and exclaimed:

"— Gaze upon her! Is she a slave?

"And then, without waiting for a response, he ran to kneel before Sarah who, trembling before him, knew not whether to meet his gaze or to flee.

"— Do not shun me, Sarah, he cried. Do you not see that now I am the one who obeys my father? I forgive you for leaving me the other day: you must have suffered greatly! Father—he continued, summoning the sacred authority of prayer—command her to bid me farewell.

"— Adieu, Edwin! she said faintly.

"Her eyes, misted over with tears, could no longer locate Edwin on the mountainside when she looked again. She leaned motionlessly against the window frame like a young vine seeking to cling to a trellis. Her soul had yielded completely to the force of a crushing blow. In her mind, Edwin was already far away, crossing the seas to Europe.

"—This is how they took my father away! she thought. Arsène, you described it well. Look, Mother, look at me: are our situations not the same? Is this not the same pain that led you to your death, one that you bore without regrets? For with death, the pain ends; one does not bring pain to heaven, where you now reside. How good you are, Mother! Do I hear you calling me?

"She had not stirred from the place where she last saw Edwin, when Mr. Primrose reappeared. He seemed distracted, and she thought he was irritated. He was not. All day he had watched with compassion as she attempted to suppress her tears or endeavored to hold open a book she could not see to read. To console her, he made sure that she could hear him ask the servants to ready Edwin's rooms for his approaching return. He heard Sarah's book drop. When he turned towards her, her clasped hands and the eyes she fixed upon him seemed to say, I owe you my life!

"— What is life without happiness? thought Mr. Primrose as he left. Poor Sarah, so obedient and gentle . . . Oh my dear family! Oh, the vow I made to you on your deathbed, Jenny! I want to fulfill my promise, yet I have said and will say again: Poor Sarah!

"Yet this pity came at the very moment when her happiness had been restored. Silent, motionless, unable to fully comprehend the happy news that summoned her back to life, she felt the blood race to her heart and bathe it in joy. At length she arose to gaze out at the sea from atop the mountain.

"— From there, she said, he will soon return, and I will see him again. So I will not die. No, Mother, I no longer desire death. He will return! His father said that his return approaches, which must mean tomorrow . . . or tonight! Searching for him already with her eyes, she thought for a moment that she saw him beneath the tamarisk trees, bent low enough by a stormy wind to touch the sand of the shoreline.

"The following day she was blessed by the same feeling of ecstasy.

"Awaiting Edwin, she felt loved by angels!

"Three more days passed, and this happy waiting slowly turned to bitter agony. Of all life's short-lived joys, the pleasure of waiting is perhaps the most fleeting. First it fills the soul with the happiness it promises. Soon it brings tender torment to the heart. Then it turns into the burning anguish that now devoured Sarah. Her darkest fears compounded her anguish when a hurricane, only a threat the day before, suddenly shook the entire island with devastating violence. The day became dark as night. Uprooted trees and the slaves' cabins and boats were hurled against the rocks by a sea that seemed furious at being unable to wreak total destruction. The slaves on the shore attempting to convey their masters' orders, the agitation of the port where ships were trying in vain to enter: such

68

scenes, viewed from the mountain, filled the soul with terror. Sarah joined her hands in prayer and lifted them to heaven, experiencing for the first time the horror and pity of an approaching shipwreck.

"Yet on other occasions she had seen the anger of nature, which returns to devastate our peaceful island almost every year. The hottest season here, known as the *hivernage*, is also the most disastrous. As in a flood of biblical magnitude, earthquakes overturn almost all the houses. Our own home has been thus destroyed twice in my lifetime. One of the most dreadful natural disasters is drought, which can last for two or three months. At that time we drink only the water carefully collected in cisterns. But sometimes they are depleted before rain, more precious than gold, returns to assuage our fears and the torments of thirst. Although fruit of course provides some relief, it also becomes scarce when the ravaging winds parch and tear apart everything in their path during the dry season.

"Sarah, whose soul was as agitated as the waves she saw in the distance, held back her sighs and almost her breath itself for fear of murmuring Edwin's name. But the terror painted on her face could not escape the good Mr. Primrose, who, when he saw the gentle, pious movement of her lips, said:

"— Pray, Sarah, for those who are in danger. At least there is nothing to fear for my son, whose short voyage would have taken scarcely two days and who must have landed safely there yesterday morning. If you look at me, you can see that Edwin is safe, for I am less worried than you.

"— Bless you for taking pity on me! said Sarah; and the tears that she had held back began to flow freely. Oh! How I will pray for you when you are on the terrifying seas! For is it not true that you will soon depart with Edwin? I will stay, I will watch, I will pray, for there will be nothing more for me to do than to pray for you and for Edwin.

"She stopped, as if alarmed at having dared to speak of Edwin before his father. Mr. Primrose, whose eyes were moistened with tears, said gently:

"— You are so good, Sarah! Verily, your submission to your duty is complete."

The Shipwreck

"A thought struck Sarah suddenly once she had retreated to her room that evening. She had not seen Arsène coming or going about the plantation all day. She vaguely remembered his last words to her before he left. She was tempted to call out to him, but a secret fear stopped her. Calm followed the confusion that had spread throughout the island during the day, and a deep silence now settled over the landscape. Too worried to sleep, and feeling both timid and bold, as she had earlier that day, Sarah went out alone to Arsène's cabin. She found it overturned by the morning's storm. There was no sign of Arsène nearby. She called out softly several times, and heard in response only the plaintive coos of the wood pigeons and the harsh cries of seabirds. Arsène surely must have profited from Silvain's departure to carry out the plan that he had only started to explain to her. As there was still a bit of moonlight, she sought to confirm her intuition by going down to where Arsène normally sheltered his canoe from inclement weather between two rocks. Not finding it, she concluded that the faithful black man had set off on a voyage. This new proof of his devotion saddened her. Without him, she felt more abandoned and vulnerable to further misfortunes. Thinking he might still be nearby, she repeated several times, 'Arsène! Arsène!' At last, she thought she heard him answer; then she thought it must be her own echo, for this voice was as weak as hers. But when she stopped calling, the sound of the voice resumed. She found her way fearfully to the foot of the cliffs from which the voice seemed to be coming. There she saw the distinct form of a black child kneeling beside a man who lay on the shore. At first she withdrew in horror. But realizing that some unfortunate soul might be in need of help, she took courage and asked:

"— Who is there?

"— Me! the child answered.

"— Who are you?

71

"— I'm Dominique, a little black child, he answered, and this is my white master, who has been sleeping for a long time. Don't be afraid, lady, my master is good, and I am little Dominique.

"She came closer. Leaning over to look at the white man, who failed to awaken, she judged that he had fainted, despite the child's assertion that he was sleeping.[8]

"— Oh! Pray tell me, how long has he been sleeping, and where did you two come from?

"— From the sea. We fell into the sea and then had to swim to land because our boat broke apart. The waves threw us here. I also slept from the fatigue of the hard landing, but my master does not awaken! I call out his name loudly and wait for him to answer.

"— Let us hope that he will hear you! said Sarah, raising the disheveled head of the shipwrecked man onto her lap. I fear he may be . . . How cold he is! Breathe on his hands and chest to warm him. God help us! If only we could wake him.

"The breath and caresses of the little black boy finally brought his master back to his senses. He opened his eyes, but closed them again immediately, as if exhausted by this first effort. Sarah, trembling with hope, told the

---

[8] The child's mistaken apprehension of his shipwrecked master's unconscious state as sleep echoes a poem by Desbordes-Valmore in which a shipwrecked slave interprets his master's death as sleep: "La veillée du nègre" (1: 115).

boy to wait while she went to seek help. —Have pity on us! Pity! cried the child as he watched her run off, and pity gave her feet wings. In a few moments, the entire plantation was awake.

"Mr. Primrose was informed that Sarah had heard cries for help down on the rocks. He got up quickly and saw to the lighting of torches and the packing of stretchers. He and several slaves then followed Sarah down to the shore, where they found the man and the child. The injured man was unable to rise, although he opened his eyelids from time to time. Once at the house, however, the care he received restored his health within a few hours.

"Mr. Primrose thanked Sarah tenderly for having awakened him on this occasion and sent her off to get some rest while he kept watch over the rescued man. But how could she sleep, preoccupied as she was with thoughts of Edwin, of the man she had just saved, and of her poor missing Arsène, who was perhaps exposed for her sake to the same dangers that very day! Several times during the night, she got up to question the blacks who were watching with their master; they all responded that the stranger was resting comfortably. But Arsène was not there.

"The next day, Mr. Primrose received his guest's assurances of his profound gratitude. The civility of his manners, his noble and solemn demeanor, redoubled Mr. Primrose's joy at having been able to help him.

"— I thought I saw a woman among the people surrounding me last night, said the stranger.

"— Oh yes!" cried the little black boy, from the corner where he had been sleeping, a white girl as lovely as a white zombie!"

"It was from this comment that, thereafter, the blacks who were present that day kept this name for Sarah.

"— That was a young girl from my household, said Mr. Primrose. It was she who first heard sounds of distress.

"— Ah, a young girl! Yes, it was a young girl, repeated the stranger, passing his hand over his forehead as if he was trying to remember. Does she belong to you, sir? I would like to thank her also.

"— She is here; you will see her shortly. God, who wanted to make use of her to save you, had kept her awake while the rest of us were sleeping. She is a child with a very sensitive soul.

"— A child! repeated the stranger again . . . I saw . . . I thought I saw a woman . . . I was confused.

"When Sarah appeared before him, he looked at her for a long time, strangely preoccupied.

"— I owe you a great deal, he said to her. I owe you my life, and more than that: a moment of happiness. Young lady, may heaven watch over you and cover you with the mercies so rarely granted to those like you. Your fortunate father says that you are sensitive, as I myself have learned.

"Sarah timidly raised her eyes to Mr. Primrose. The name 'father,' which he did not deny, made her shiver and blush.

"Several days passed before the stranger was able to leave his room. He watched Sarah silently, sighing often.

"Mr. Primrose, who guessed that he suffered from a spiritual affliction, felt a strong empathic bond. Several exchanges between the two men, which would have been vague for any other listener, soon revealed to him that profound grief darkened the existence of his new friend. Such at least, without having uttered the word, was the title he gave the stranger in his own mind. Although he wanted to know his guest better, the attentions he bestowed upon the stranger were not intermingled with questions. He knew only that two years ago the stranger had been recalled to Dominica[9] by his father's death, and that he had spent his youth in Europe.

"The traveler added: My father left me nothing but gold. My dearest hopes are dashed; all the gold my father possessed cannot revive them. For two years, I have been wandering aimlessly through life, useful to no one, with no other goal than to distract myself and to escape bitter memories.

---

[9] Dominica is an island located between Martinique and Guadeloupe.

"Mr. Primrose felt profound empathy for this man, whose story seemed so like his own.

"Mr. Primrose was also saddened to learn of Arsène's flight. The poor black was, in his mind, an ingrate, for Mr. Primrose had always treated him with kindness. He knew nothing of his manager's severe treatment of Arsène. He called Sarah and questioned her about the black man's strange departure. Sarah answered that she truly had no idea of his whereabouts, but that she was deeply worried about him.

"— If he desired to leave, said Mr. Primrose, why did he not ask me? I would have granted his request. You should understand that I did not consider him a slave, and that he was not among those I sold with my other goods. I wanted him to be as free as he was when he arrived here with you.

"As he said this, he handed a document to her.

"Sarah, greatly surprised, hardly knew what to say as she read quickly through the list of the slaves sold by Silvain.

"— Here is Arsène's name, she said, among those of the other slaves.

"— You have my solemn word, Mr. Primrose exclaimed with astonishment, that Silvain expressly disobeyed me, for I forbade him to do just this. I would have corrected this possibly involuntary error. But poor Arsène has freed himself. I had already acknowledged his freedom. I will not reproach him for his actions. We need never speak of the matter again."

A Betrayal

"For two days Mr. Primrose waited anxiously for Edwin's return. At last, having impatiently directed his spyglass toward the point on the horizon where he expected his son to eventually appear, he thought he saw a sail. Sarah, watching him closely, saw the sudden joy expressed on his face. As soon as he had moved away from the window, she ran to it and, looking with her heart instead of the spyglass, perceived the sail of Edwin's small boat. In the next moment she believed she saw Edwin himself stretching out his arms in the distance.

"The stranger, to whom Sarah had previously appeared pale and pensive, was struck by her joyful look and heightened color as she ran into Mr. Primrose's room, crying:

"— It is he! I recognize him. He is nearly here. He is just arriving in the port. Oh! I have seen him.

"He was amazed at how greatly she loved her brother. They all returned to the window. But, even with the aid of the spyglass, Mr. Primrose was still unable to discern his son.

"As the stranger prepared to accompany Mr. Primrose, who was hastening to the shore, he saw that Sarah hesitated as to whether to join their company or not. He took her by the hand to lead her to meet this cherished brother. Mr. Primrose, who continued his hurried descent, had not forbidden her to come, and Sarah let herself be led along silently and without resistance.

"They were only a third of the way down the mountain path when they saw Edwin dashing toward them. Pale and breathless, he threw himself into his father's arms and managed only to gasp:

"— Where is Sarah?

"— My son! responded his father, I hope that at least your second thought will be for me.

"— My life is for you, said Edwin, my terror for her.

"— What terror, dear Edwin? Do you not see her coming down to meet you?

"— Oh! Yes, I see her, he said, grasping her hands and then falling back into his father's arms. His father, surprised by his unseemly behavior, was going to reproach him for it, when Edwin burst out, Why did Silvain leave Sainte-Marie without me? Did you order him to leave me there, Father? How could you betray my obedience, precisely when I had yielded so respectfully to your wishes?

"— I fail to understand, my son. Where is Silvain?

"— Is he not here? asked Edwin with renewed concern.

"— No, he is not here, replied Mr. Primrose.

"— Not here! And not in Sainte-Marie! Then the scoundrel has fled!

"— Dare you proclaim his guilt, Edwin! If your accusation is unjust, how will you repair the harm you have done? Has pity turned to furor in your heart?

"— A curse on the monster who betrayed you, said Edwin. He fled, I tell you. He left the island during the night, taking your entire fortune with him. You see that my hatred, and the Swede's fears, were justified.

"Mr. Primrose remained composed although he was now seized by a horrible suspicion. He hurried his son toward home, where they could further clarify this appalling mystery in private.

"The stranger, who understood neither the son's exclamations nor the father's confusion, dared not join in the scene of desolation that was unfolding. He returned to his own room, almost as worried as his unfortunate friends.

"The clarifications provided in the course of their conversation only confirmed their worst fears.

"As soon as the perfidious manager saw that he had Mr. Primrose's treasure in his possession, he pretended to go off to alert the captain who had brought them from Saint-Barthélemy that he should prepare for their imminent return. Instead, he disappeared with the ship. The captain was no doubt his accomplice. Their departure had taken place at an early hour, when most people were still sleeping. —But I was kept awake by the idea of seeing you again, continued Edwin, and thus I confidently awaited Silvain, thinking that this terrible day would be one of the best of my life. You can imagine my impatience when the whole morning had gone by without Silvain's return! Yielding at last to my agitation, I ran to the harbor, where I searched in vain for the ship that had been lying ready for us the previous evening. My first thought—a guilty one—was that this traitor had abandoned me by your own instructions until, alone and without Sarah, you would come to get me. I was overwhelmed with sorrow and berated myself (forgive me, Father!) for having trusted your words. I returned to the Swede's house, convinced that he knew of your plans. My thoughts were in such disarray that I was hardly able to tell him of Silvain's sudden disappearance or of the grief and anger that overwhelmed me. But instead of confirming his knowledge of the scheme, as I had expected, he was as surprised as I had been earlier. I soon realized from his reaction that he had good reasons to fear for your welfare, oh my God, a horrifying notion that I had at first rejected. My fears were all focused on Sarah, whom I supposed would now be prey to this appalling man's persecutions. As I was unable to gather any other information about this inexplicable disappearance, I left that very day, assisted by the Swede, who trembles for us and deplores the betrayal of your admirable confidence and charitable trust.

"Upon Edwin's recital of these sad details, Mr. Primrose sank into his chair like a man who had been dealt a fatal blow.

"Edwin, his only child, was thus stripped of his héritage, through his father's fault! With despairing eyes, Mr. Primrose held out his shaking hands, able to utter no words other than:

"— Forgive me, my dear son!

"Even Edwin's sobs, his tender embraces, the kisses he lavished on his father's furrowed brow, could not wrench his father out of his profound and solitary suffering.

"— Father, repeated Edwin, my beloved father! Take hold of yourself. I kneel at your feet. If you let me perish from sadness, who will console you? Listen! You have not lost everything! I am here. I will work, Father! My strength, my youth, my life, are all yours; but if you love me, speak to me. Banish from your face this sadness that shatters my soul and my courage!

"Unable to speak, Mr. Primrose threw his arms around Edwin's neck and pressed him against his chest, groaning heavily.

"Sarah had not uttered a word. She had not added her own tears or caresses to Edwin's consolations. Pale and mute, she had gone out suddenly, leaving each man to seek solace in the other's embrace.

"Mr. Primrose noticed her absence with astonishment. Heartsick at Silvain's base ingratitude, he could not help feeling bitterness upon noticing that Sarah was no longer there.

"— How can it be? he exclaimed. At this moment of our greatest disaster, she abandons us without a word, without a sign of concern for our fate! And Arsène has already fled. Oh Edwin—he continued with a sad smile—I am loved by you alone.

"— Father! Edwin protested, Wherever she is, she loves you and is grieving for you!

Sarah Makes Herself a Slave

"Sarah was not crying. Her sorrow was so great that it dried her tears. One resolve had taken hold of her passionate soul. Edwin's exclamation "I will work, Father!" had found an echo in her and revealed her duty. Without reflection, without advice, without any guide other than her love for Edwin's father, she started out, drawn by a sudden inspiration, and made her way to the stranger's door. Surrounded by darkness, seated in a darkened room, he was lost in thought about the turbulent events transpiring around him. He recognized Sarah with trepidation.

"— Sir, she began, approaching him with a timid and troubled countenance, I have come to ask you . . .

"She then stopped, no longer sure of how to express her thoughts.

"— What is it? he asked, in a voice that invited trust.

82

"After a moment, Sarah began to speak again, trembling, but with an endearing candor.

"— Sir, are you very rich?

"— Too much so, replied the stranger, for my wealth has made me wretched.

"— In that case, she went on, could you, would you be willing to buy a slave, a poor abandoned girl, a lost child who would serve you and give her poor life to you to save her benefactor, who has been betrayed and impoverished by an evil man? Sir, I am this child, this slave on her knees before you. I am not the daughter of the man who saved you, yes, who saved you! she said in a voice of celestial respect. Oh, if you are truly rich, buy Sarah for a very high price to save Mr. Primrose, for he is the best of men!

"She would have continued her persuasive speech if her listener's surprise and emotion had not prompted him to interrupt her. The sight of this young girl kneeling before him, of her deep sorrow, and of this resolution—so simple and sublime in its objective, so apparently inconsistent with the elevation of her soul—astonished him in a manner that Sarah took for a refusal.

"— She hid her face in despair and said, So I am turned away even as a slave!

"— No, said the stranger, no, you are not being turned away. At last I can thank you for having saved my life, which, now that it is no longer useless for others, becomes bearable for me. Your good deed will be repaid, if it can be. Yes, Sarah, I am rich (and for the first time, I forgive my father his wealth and I bless him); yes, in truth, I am rich! he cried joyfully. And from this moment on, you are too. Your devotion, Sarah, will not be wasted; it is as beautiful as you are. Poor Mr. Primrose—he added as an afterthought—your greatest loss is not being the father of such a girl!

"— He is Edwin's father, sir! Edwin will stay by his father's side. What does Mr. Primrose have to regret when his son is there with him! I will go with you, sir. I will serve you, I promise . . . No, I will never cry over my separation from them!

"And her tears flowed abundantly.

"— But, lovely Sarah, can you leave this brother, or at least he whom I thought of as your brother, this Edwin, so worthy of being loved, for me?

"— I would have had to leave him anyway, sir, upon his father's order. I am just a poor orphan whom he could send away at any time. This approaching separation was to have been the proof of my submission. Instead, thanks to you, sir, it will be the proof of my gratitude. You have made it easier for me to leave.

"— And was it easy for him to leave you, Sarah?

"— Easy! cried the poor child. Oh, sir!— After a brief silence, she continued: But I was not worthy of being Mr. Primrose's daughter, because, without the tender pity he had for me, I would have been all along what I will now joyfully become through an act of my own will.

"Her soul was truly flooded at that moment with the profound joy that results from a great sacrifice made for a loved one.

"The stranger, more moved by Sarah's sacrifice than he appeared to be, forced himself to bring the interview to an end by affirming that on the morrow she would receive the price of her freedom, to be given to Mr. Primrose.

"— It is you, Sarah, who should offer it to him; you are perhaps the only one from whom he would accept such a gift.

"Sarah then left the man she now regarded as her master. And before falling asleep, she thanked God for the name 'slave' that she had previously regarded with such horror.

"The next day, at the first light of dawn, she arose. The stranger sent little Dominique to fetch her, and she returned with him almost immediately. When the stranger saw her come in, he wordlessly signed over to her half of his great wealth, which covered the losses Mr. Primrose had suffered. Sarah lowered her eyes in silence while he examined her intently.

"— Do you not even choose to read this document that binds you to me forever? he asked. I pray that through it I can repay my debt to you and to Mr. Primrose.

"She pressed her lips to the document with respect. —My life is not worth the price you are willing to pay for it! Oh, sir, how fortunate you are, she said with heartfelt emotion, to be able to give everything!

"— You underestimate yourself, he replied. May others appreciate you as I do!

"They planned then how to prevent Mr. Primrose from rejecting this selfless gift. Sarah worried that the sole means for gaining his assent was to leave before he discovered her sacrifice. They continued talking, uncertain and agitated.

Meanwhile in a storm of emotion Edwin precipitously entered the room where his father had spent a sleepless night. His father looked at him with great concern, not daring to ask what had unleashed this new distress.

"— What is it, he said, marshaling all his strength. "What even sadder thing could have occurred? Answer me, Edwin. What news do you bring me?

"— Appalling news, said Edwin, whose whole body shuddered as he spoke. Sarah! Father, Sarah!"

"— Yes? Sarah? Where is Sarah?

"— Sold! Sold for you! A slave! And forever lost to me!

"— Son, said Mr. Primrose, growing pale, spare me! Tell me that I have misunderstood you, or that your misfortune has disturbed your mind!

"— It has disturbed her mind, Father! She sold herself to restore to us what Silvain stole! She has a master!— Edwin fell almost lifeless on his father's bed.

"— Where is Sarah? Let someone call Sarah! cried Mr. Primrose, as overwhelmed as his son. Sarah! Sarah!

"And soon Sarah's name was ringing out in every corner of the house.

Sarah ran to this cherished and powerful voice. Seeing Mr. Primrose's unprecedented distress, she fell to her knees, crying, Mercy!, as if she were guilty.

"— Foolish child! What have you done? said Mr. Primrose in a stifled voice. Do you not know that you could cause the death to those you love by thus immolating yourself for them? What have you done? Explain the mystery that could prove to be my son's death knell.

"Horrified, Sarah hid her head in shame.

"— Sir, cried the stranger, drawn out of his room by the commotion, listen to me first. You are devastating this child; look at her!

"— Good and tender girl! said Mr. Primrose, raising her up from the ground where she lay, come let me look at you! Yes—he continued with transport—let me gaze upon an angel, one of the few who still exist in this unhappy world. Oh! Come, my child, for I love you like Edwin despite the harm you are doing him.

"And leading her by the arm to the side of his son, he said:

"— Here she is, Edwin, I give her to you.— He guided her gently to the desperate young man, whose eyes closed as he received her in his arms.

87

"— Sir, Mr. Primrose said more calmly now to the traveler who stood watching them silently, judge for yourself if this young woman, whom I place in the arms of my son, is a slave. She now becomes inseparable from me as well. No one can dispute my paternal rights. I take on the title of father before you and before heaven.

"— Is it possible, then, said the stranger, seizing Mr. Primrose's hands and pressing them ardently between his own, that you can refuse, that you would reject the blessed testimony of your daughter's love? For from this moment on, I swear before heaven, as you have, that she is as rich as I am. Here is the proof—he added, taking from Sarah's hands the paper that she had been hiding with mortal fear.— This is not a certificate of enslavement, sir, it is an act of legal recognition, because I knew, or at least I assumed, that Sarah could not be a slave.

"And there, in her presence, he related all that she had said and done the previous evening. Mr. Primrose's eyes moistened with tenderness as he looked at his young pupil, whose exquisite modesty was no less touching than his son's intoxicated joy.

"In the first moments of the drama, he had forgotten that he was ruined. He thought only of Sarah and rejoiced that he would no longer be required to abandon her. Emerging from a combat that had cost his heart dearly, he thanked fate for obliging him to forget England and the brilliant marriage planned for his son. But now, holding the document in his hands, he remembered his situation. The momentary reprieve he had enjoyed was dissipated. The look he cast on Edwin showed both his deep gratitude and the insurmountable pride that urged him to reject the godsend he had received. Edwin acknowledged his father's feelings with an involuntary movement. Stepping away from Sarah, he sadly approached Mr. Primrose, who in a state of agitation, was walking around the room with bended head.

"— Father, said Edwin in a deep and altered voice, I will be no less courageous than Sarah; she has taught me to obey. Dictate my destiny.

"— My dear child! My worthy son, answered Mr. Primrose, standing before him. I can see that you want to spread balm over the deep and no doubt fatal wound inflicted upon me! Your words gratify me, my Edwin, and I feel myself dying of a remorse crying out from the depths of my conscience. You are all too generous toward a man who has verily been less prudent than this young woman.

"— Sir! interrupted Edwin, addressing the stranger. Can an honest man's error really be called a crime? A scoundrel betrays us, and his victim speaks of remorse! Defend my father, please, against himself; for I myself have no influence over him. I no longer know what to say to him, and I am so sad, I could die.

"— Your father, the stranger replied gravely, is unjust toward himself because of the excess of his love for you.

89

But he cannot persist in a refusal that belies his own word. He adopted Sarah, he gave you to her, solemnly gave her to you. Now for him to refuse the fortune she possesses would be to reject her, to say to her: I prefer death to your happiness. Such a choice would be impossible to make. Pride in virtue does not extend that far. No, sir, you will not be so cruel. You will have compassion for two precious children sent to you by the love of Providence. And if the voice of an unfortunate man can have any influence over your soul—he added, clasping him with all his strength—then let me add it to their tears. I ask you to have pity and grant happiness to a life that you have saved."

Arsène Returns

"While within the house Sarah's and Edwin's fate was being decided, at the door to the plantation house a crowd had assembled to embrace and question Arsène, who had just arrived. He had come back in a happy state of mind. He had learned of favorable changes occurring on the island of Dominica, whence he came to apologize for his flight and to console his young mistress. All the blacks were very fond of him, and they had rushed forth, joyfully raising their voices to greet him and celebrate his return. After the first outbursts of their simple friendship, they told him of Mr. Primrose's misfortunes and Silvain's evil deeds. They all considered the overseer to be *mazulitapan*,[10] an invective the poor slaves used against their torturers.

"Arsène was moved by their stories. But nothing could express his frenetic anger upon learning that Sarah had sold herself the previous evening and was soon to leave. Dominique had heard the news about Sarah; and with a heart heavy with grief for the beautiful white girl, he had come to tell the other blacks that the lovely zombie had made herself the slave of his master. Edwin too had learned about Sarah's decision from Dominique in the morning. The extraordinary news had been making the rounds of all the groups of blacks, when Arsène reappeared in their midst. Arsène could not have been more stunned by what he was hearing than if the sky had fallen. He leaped and darted about through the shocked assembly, yelling at the top of his lungs like a man possessed. Edwin, hearing his cries, thought that the blacks were beginning a revolt on the plantation. He hurried out from his father's house and

---

[10] Mazulitapan, also spelled Masulipatnam or Machilipatnam, is a region, near Yanoan, on the coast of Coromandel in India near the former French colony of Pondicherry. Desbordes-Valmore's interesting use of the term as a name used by slaves to denote cruel slave masters may be related to the history of the French colonial governor Joseph François Dupleix in Mazulitapan. Dupleix was known for such brutality that he was recalled by the French government in 1754. He returned to France with members of his colonial guard, easily recognizable by their white scarves of Mazulitapan silk. Some of these soldiers joined the French navy and eventually settled in the Caribbean, where they may have become known for brutal practices like those cultivated by Dupleix in India.

saw Arsène running around, yelling, his arms outstretched to the sky. Edwin called him to his side. The black man followed him to the room where Sarah, Mr. Primrose, and the stranger were all assembled. Ready to expire at Sarah's knees, he could barely utter the words:

"— A slave! No, never a slave! White and free, free like her mother! Oh, bad little mistress! Have you thus forgotten everything Arsène explained to you?

"— At the name 'Arsène,' the stranger, who had been examining him curiously, bounded toward him, raised him to his feet with great haste, and exclaimed loudly:

"—Arsène, Arsène! Where is Narcisse?

"This name, this voice, this sudden apparition nearly rendered Arsène senseless. Staring desperately at the man asking the question, he gestured at Sarah and said in a voice of extreme emotion:

"— Here is Narcisse!

"And then he fell in a faint at their feet.

"For a moment all was confusion and disorder; everyone talked at the same time and no one understood anything that was said. The stranger, more tormented than the others, sought to recall his slave to life, and devoured Sarah with his eyes. Sarah was crying and pressing Arsène's icy hands in hers.

"— Oh! Speak to me, he finally said with a deathly anxiety. What did he mean? Do you know Narcisse? Could it be that she still lives? Speak to me, where is Narcisse?

"— She is no longer, answered Sarah. I no longer remember her; but Arsène has told me that she was my mother.

"The man's face expressed expectation and pain, doubt and anguish simultaneously. He dared not yet embrace a daughter whose existence he had never imagined. Arsène alone could shatter or fulfill the sudden presentiment of this miracle, and Arsène's unconscious state affected him with an inexpressible anxiety.

"The good black man, having by degrees regained his senses and his reason, thought he was in heaven upon finding himself thus caressed by those he loved most. His initial exaltation made his words so confused that it was impossible to discern in them anything but an overwhelming joy, almost alarming for those watching over him. Finally, when his emotions had settled, he satisfied his master's impatient expectation by recounting the same story he had already told to Sarah. Narcisse's husband heard this story with many tears; but Narcisse had sent him a daughter, and this daughter was the living image of her mother.

"Mr. Primrose no longer dared counter the wishes of this man who had been unhappy for such a long time and who beseeched him not to destroy this reprieve, so dearly purchased. He yielded, sacrificing pride to tenderness. And a few days later, Sarah gave both men the title 'father,' at the same time that she received the sweet name 'daughter.'

"What became of them?" I asked Eugénie with interest when she had ceased speaking.

She gestured toward the isle of shades.

"They are all there," she said. "After having lived together for so long, they lie in rest together also, so that they will never be separated."

"I think they are very fortunate," I said, looking off at the melancholy island in the distance. For the first time the idea of death did not terrify me.

The piercing sound of a fife brought us back abruptly from our reverie. Eugénie brightened and grabbed me by the hand, leading me back to the town where the music signaled the retreat to the fort constructed on a neighboring cliff. I noted with surprise that the musician was masked, and that he ran dancing ahead of the marching drummer. This spectacle, new for me, helped lift my somber mood as well, and we began to run along to the bright invitation of this tune.

All the young Creole girls ran to meet us, and then began to disperse to their homes, scattered here and there along the flanks of the mountain.

We had come now to the entrance to the town, and Eugénie, who was in a hurry to rejoin her mother, bade me farewell while showing me the quickest path to return to my home. She then disappeared among the darkening rocks, while I remained alone at the shore, almost frightened by the shadows blurring the sea into the horizon. Then the moon, which had been veiled by clouds for a moment, reappeared with such brilliance that I walked rapidly and fearlessly along the bank. I was feeling completely reassured when I saw two people sitting on the stones of the beach. I was immediately curious to see what they were watching so attentively, perched there just beyond the reach of the waves, so absorbed that they were oblivious to my approach. Their postures seemed as sad as their features were lovely. It was a young girl and an equally young man. Their eyes were fixed on two crowns of white acacia blossoms that the movement of the sea was pulling toward an island. I recognized it as the asylum of the dead. While the young girl drew more flower petals from among the blossoms that adorned her breast and tossed them after the crowns, the young man, who seemed to be her brother, wove other flowers into his sister's wavy black hair. At length, the girl lifted her lowered gaze to meet the eyes of the young man who was now standing before her. Still silent, he led her by the hand toward a dwelling, half hidden by two aged tamarind trees, that I had not noticed before.

Once more alone, I began to be carried away again by my imagination. Despite myself, I furtively glanced over and over at the coast of that uninhabited island, where I thought I saw ghosts walking slowly in the starlight. The frightful cry of a wild bird banished the last vestiges of my courage, and I began to run in earnest, promising myself to ask Eugénie about the two charming creatures who had reminded me of Edwin and Sarah.

The next day at dawn, I heard someone knocking on the wooden shutters to my room. I awoke precipitously, sure that it was Eugénie who, as was her wont, had come to awaken me to watch the first rays of the rising sun. I opened the door, and we walked up the steep hillside, talking about my encounter of the previous evening. Eugénie promised to tell me everything I wanted to know. "But," she said, "do you only want to hear our island's sad stories? You will want to leave. I think I should keep still!"

"No," I answered, hugging her; "we will keep sharing stories until sundown."

She threw her arms around my neck to thank me. That very evening, I learned the story of another adventure that often comes back to my memory, and that I would like to tell just as she related it.

Works Cited in the Notes

Desbordes-Valmore, Marceline. *Les œuvres poétiques de Marceline Desbordes-Valmore*. Ed. Marc Bertrand. 2 vols. Grenbole: PU de Grenoble, 1973.

Descourtilz, Michel-Etienne. *Voyages d'un naturaliste*. 3 vols. Paris: Dufart, 1809.

Modern Language Association of America
Texts and Translations

Texts

Anna Banti. *"La signorina" e altri racconti*. Ed. and introd. Carol Lazzaro-Weis. 2001.

Adolphe Belot. *Mademoiselle Giraud, ma femme*. Ed and introd. Christopher Rivers. 2002.

Dovid Bergelson. אָפּגאַנג. Ed. and introd. Joseph Sherman. 1999.

Elsa Bernstein. *Dämmerung: Schauspiel in fünf Akten*. Ed. and introd. Susanne Kord. 2003.

Edith Bruck. *Lettera alla madre*. Ed. and introd. Gabriella Romani. 2006.

Isabelle de Charrière. *Lettres de Mistriss Henley publiées par son amie*. Ed. Joan Hinde Stewart and Philip Stewart. 1993.

Isabelle de Charrière. *Trois femmes: Nouvelle de l'Abbé de la Tour*. Ed. and introd. Emma Rooksby. 2007.

François-Timoléon de Choisy, Marie-Jeanne L'Héritier, and Charles Perrault. *Histoire de la Marquise-Marquis de Banneville*. Ed. Joan DeJean. 2004.

Sophie Cottin. *Claire d'Albe*. Ed. and introd. Margaret Cohen. 2002.

Marceline Desbordes-Valmore. *Sarah*. Ed. Deborah Jenson and Doris Y. Kaddish. 2008.

Claire de Duras. *Ourika*. Ed. Joan DeJean. Introd. DeJean and Margaret Waller. 1994.

Şeyh Galip. *Hüsn ü Aşk*. Ed. and introd. Victoria Rowe Holbrook. 2005.

Françoise de Graffigny. *Lettres d'une Péruvienne*. Introd. Joan DeJean and Nancy K. Miller. 1993.

Sofya Kovalevskaya. *Нигилистка*. Ed. and introd. Natasha Kolchevska. 2001.

Thérèse Kuoh-Moukoury. *Rencontres essentielles*. Introd. Cheryl Toman. 2002.

Juan José Millás. *"Trastornos de carácter" y otros cuentos*. Introd. Pepa Anastasio. 2007.

Emilia Pardo Bazán. *"El encaje roto" y otros cuentos*. Ed. and introd. Joyce Tolliver. 1996.

Rachilde. *Monsieur Vénus: Roman matérialiste*. Ed. and introd. Melanie Hawthorne and Liz Constable. 2004.

Marie Riccoboni. *Histoire d'Ernestine*. Ed. Joan Hinde Stewart and Philip Stewart. 1998.

Eleonore Thon. *Adelheit von Rastenberg*. Ed. and introd. Karin A. Wurst. 1996.

Translations

Anna Banti. *"The Signorina" and Other Stories*. Trans. Martha King and Carol Lazzaro-Weis. 2001.

Adolphe Belot. *Mademoiselle Giraud, My Wife*. Trans. Christopher Rivers. 2002.

Dovid Bergelson. *Descent*. Trans. Joseph Sherman. 1999.

Elsa Bernstein. *Twilight: A Drama in Five Acts*. Trans. Susanne Kord. 2003.

Edith Bruck. *Letter to My Mother*. Trans. Brenda Webster with Gabriella Romani. 2006.

Isabelle de Charrière. *Letters of Mistress Henley Published by Her Friend*. Trans. Philip Stewart and Jean Vaché. 1993.

Isabelle de Charrière. *Three Women: A Novel by the Abbé de la Tour*. Trans. Emma Rooksby. 2007.

François-Timoléon de Choisy, Marie-Jeanne L'Héritier, and Charles Perrault. *The Story of the Marquise-Marquis de Banneville*. Trans. Steven Rendall. 2004.

Sophie Cottin. *Claire d'Albe*. Trans. Margaret Cohen. 2002.

Marceline Desbordes-Valmore. *Sarah*. Trans. Deborah Jenson and Doris Y. Kaddish. 2008.

Claire de Duras. *Ourika*. Trans. John Fowles. 1994.

Şeyh Galip. *Beauty and Love*. Trans. Victoria Rowe Holbrook. 2005.

Françoise de Graffigny. *Letters from a Peruvian Woman*. Trans. David Kornacker. 1993.

Sofya Kovalevskaya. *Nihilist Girl*. Trans. Natasha Kolchevska with Mary Zirin. 2001.

Thérèse Kuoh-Moukoury. *Essential Encounters*. Trans. Cheryl Toman. 2002.

Juan José Millás. *"Personality Disorders" and Other Stories*. Trans. Gregory B. Kaplan. 2007.

Emilia Pardo Bazán. *"Torn Lace" and Other Stories*. Trans. María Cristina Urruela. 1996.

Rachilde. *Monsieur Vénus: A Materialist Novel*. Trans. Melanie Hawthorne. 2004.

Marie Riccoboni. *The Story of Ernestine.* Trans. Joan Hinde Stewart and Philip Stewart. 1998.

Eleonore Thon. *Adelheit von Rastenberg.* Trans. George F. Peters. 1996.

Texts and Translations in One Volume

انتخاب کا شاعری اردو جدید / *An Anthology of Modern Urdu Poetry.* Ed., introd., and trans. M. A. R. Habib. 2003.

An Anthology of Spanish American Modernismo. Ed. Kelly Washbourne. Trans. Washbourne with Sergio Waisman. 2007.

An Anthology of Nineteenth-Century Women's Poetry from France. Ed. Gretchen Schultz. Trans. Anne Atik, Michael Bishop, Mary Ann Caws, Melanie Hawthorne, Rosemary Lloyd, J. S. A. Lowe, Laurence Porter, Christopher Rivers, Schultz, Patricia Terry, and Rosanna Warren. 2008.